Sydney & Connor

Ho! Ho! Ho!

Merry Christmas!

Love
Grandma & Pap Sleigh
2013

Who Is Santa?

And How Did He Get To The North Pole?

Story by Stephen Bigalow

Illustrated by Bill Megenhardt

Who Is Santa?
And How Did He Get To The North Pole?

Copyright © 2013 by Stephen W. Bigalow

Printed in China
August 2013/Batch A71
ISBN: 978-0-9773757-3-8

Profit Publishing Company
39 West Trace Creek Dr.
Spring, Texas 77381

281-296-0351

ACKNOWLEDGEMENTS

The inspiration for writing a children's Christmas book stems from the good fortune of having a close and loving family. Some of my fondest childhood memories are those of sitting on the couch with my brother and me on each side of my mother as she read Christmas stories during the holiday season. I am forever grateful for the love and support of my mother June Bigalow, my brother and close friend Andrew Bigalow and his family, his wife Polly, and my nephews Drew and Clayton. I am fortunate to have had the constant support of my sister Diane Kelly and brother-in-law Frank Kelly who have been a consistent example of good family values and human integrity. Diane Kelly and my mother June Bigalow graciously contributed with constructive contributions to the storyline. My niece Nancy and nephew Jeff and their families have brought great joy to life and the holiday seasons. A special smile goes to Matt Lamirand and sons, Ben and Zach who remind me of the joys of being a child. I would like to express my appreciation to my son-in-law Patrick Hammack, his wife Melissa, and two beautiful daughters, Macey and Avery. Also, thanks to his company Anchor Digital Publishing for their creative applications to produce the book in interactive mode. I owe an immense amount of gratitude to my partner in life, my wife Sandra, who is a constant reminder of how people can make life very pleasant for others with their caring natures.

William Megenhardt is greatly appreciated for his art talents and his insights for developing a book like this. Last but definitely not least, Betsy Burnell deserves heaps of accolades for her diligent editing, being a life saver. Melissa Hammack's attentive eye and teaching background were an immeasurable assistance in the final edit. Many thanks go to members of http://www.candlestickforum.com/ for their input and support of this project.

TABLE OF CONTENTS

THE CLAUSES

Christmas is a wonderful time of year. A magical feeling develops with the anticipation of Santa Claus. Kids from 1 to 100 years old get into the spirit of the Christmas season. Households all over the world get ready for the arrival of the jolly old man. He has been called St. Nicholas, Santa Claus, Der Weihnachtsmann, Pere Noel, Sinterklaas, but whatever name is given to him, his name brings images of joy and happiness. When the decorations come out of the attic, homes take on a whole new atmosphere. Pine boughs decorate the mantle and provide the familiar Christmas smells. The Christmas tree, decorated with glittering lights and ornaments, becomes the center point of living rooms and family rooms. The sound of Christmas music, the smell of fresh baked cookies, hustle and bustle of the Christmas shopping brings a life of its own to the holiday season. All this activity is for the arrival of a jolly old man.

This jolly old man travels the world on Christmas Eve, delivering presents for all the good little boys and girls. We all know he leaves his home at the North Pole. He travels in a sleigh pulled by eight tiny reindeer. His sack can magically hold the many toys and presents for all the children in the world. His magical sleigh and his reindeer can fly. Santa himself has magical talents for getting his big chubby body down some very small chimneys. Each year, for as long as we can remember, we have anxiously awaited the arrival of Santa Claus, anticipating the arrival of the holiday season just after the last leaf has fallen.

The weather turns cold, the snowflakes fill the air, and white blankets of snow transform the appearance of our towns and homes into a wintry welcome for jolly old St. Nick.

Does cold weather ever slow him down? Heavens no!

As we all know, he spends most of the year making toys at the North Pole. But have you ever wondered how it came to be that his home and workshop are at the North Pole?

The North Pole is cold and far away! This is the story of how Santa came to live in such a faraway place. You will discover answers to many of the questions surrounding Santa. The elves, the sleigh and reindeer, Santa's magic, candy canes, hot chocolate and letters to Santa Claus. How did all these things become associated with Christmas? Lets find out together!

WHO IS SANTA?

Of course, the story has to start with Santa Claus. History books indicate he was a saint. We want to know the story of his name: St. Nicholas, St. Nick, or the name St. Klaus has evolved through the years into Santa Claus. If the definition of a saint is a good man, then Santa Claus definitely fits that description. He was a man of means but no one knows the source. He was very different from a wealthy person of many centuries ago, a time when the wealthy liked to flaunt their wealth, living in castles and having extravagant balls with horse drawn carriages.

Santa Claus did not show off his wealth. He had a nice large home and shared it often with friends. But it was not flamboyant as were the big estates or castles of the times. It was a nice solid built log home in a quiet, out of the way region and secluded in a large forest. The large log walls and heavy wooden doors kept Santa's house warm and cozy through the cold winters. Where exactly? No one seems able to recall. They know it was in the northern regions of the world. The weather was cold most of the year. This did not bother Santa or Mrs. Claus. They were both very content to be inside in a nice, warm, toasty home where their many large fireplaces kept them warm through the cold winters. Often Santa would marvel to Mrs. Claus, "Aren't we lucky to have such a nice life and such a fine home?" The lifestyle suited Santa very well. He was able to spend many, many hours at his favorite hobby, making toys. Now this was an unusual hobby. but then, Santa was a very unusual man.

Many centuries ago, the wealthy entertained themselves with foxhunts, traveling and attending fancy balls. This was not Santa. He enjoyed designing and building toys. He was very skillful at carving and he very cleverly designed toys with moving parts. He loved to make wagons, rocking horses, dolls, playhouses, any toy you could imagine. He enjoyed bringing toys to life, painting them with vibrant colors. He could work for hours at his workbench, feeling the soothing heat of the fireplace and listening to the crackling of the logs.

Mrs. Claus loved their lifestyle as well. Her favorite past-time was cooking. This, too, was an unusual interest, for the Lady of the house did not do the cooking. The Clauses could afford the helpers necessary to perform that task, but Mrs. Claus prided herself on her cooking abilities. The many hours that Santa spent making toys, Mrs. Claus spent cooking pies and cakes for dessert, turkeys and hams for meals, but most importantly, candy. Do you suppose Santa's large girth might have been caused by Mrs. Claus's constant supply of delicious food? Of course, you'll never hear Santa complain!

Although this may appear to be a somewhat secluded life, do not be fooled. The Clauses always had many guests and friends visiting. Their home was the entertainment center for many miles around. Friends would travel a great distance to come and enjoy the friendly atmosphere. Obviously, Mrs. Claus's cooking skills made for many handsome feasts. The women loved to spend time chatting and cooking in the large kitchen area. Her fireplaces and ovens were the envy of many. The men would sit and whittle, repeating the many stories of the northern forests, many of which became more embellished as the years passed.

Life was good for the Clauses but it was their kindhearted spirit that eventually caused problems for them. It would seem unusual for someone who is good spirited to have that trait become a problem. It took a few years for the situation to develop. Santa, as we have seen, was constantly making toys. Mrs. Claus was always cooking.

Fortunately, food is eaten, so it does not take up space. However, the toys Santa made had to be stored somewhere. Over a period of time, the barns were filled with toys, leaving very little space for the cattle or their feed. This became a very big problem, especially when you think about how many barns there were on the Clauses' homestead.

THE CLAUS'S NORTH FOREST HOME

To understand the space required by the toys you must be aware that Santa's Homestead was enormous. There were forests of magnificent trees which could be six feet in diameter with tree tops hundreds of feet in the air. Mild breezes make pleasant swooshing noises in the branches as they swayed against the sky. There were also very spacious, well-kept fields that produce enough food for the families and animals to last through the long cold winters. Although the house was made of solid straight logs the barns were built of stone. To make sure there was enough room for as much storage as possible for crops each year, the barns were very large.

Along with the Clauses' house and many barns, there were four other homes where the workers and their families lived. Santa's helpers were all good workers and enjoyed many benefits from the generosity of the Clauses. Adam and Sarah had been with them for many years. Eric, Adams younger brother, and Mildred, Hugo and Ingrid, Peter and Gwen all were very reliable workers. Between the families, there were twelve children ranging in age from 3 to 12 years old. All were considered by the Clauses as their extended family. The workers were not ones to ever complain, but they began to question how they were to house the animals along with their feed storage when the space in the barns was becoming less and less. Walking into any one of the barns a person saw a beautiful array of colors. Toys filled the animal stalls, hung across the walls and stacked all the way up to the ceiling! Every available square inch of space was loaded with Santa's special toys. As you might guess, the more toys in the barn, the less space for the animals and the crops. What a problem!

SANTA'S IDEA

Each evening, Santa and Mrs. Claus would have their dinners in their magnificent dining room. A roaring fire in the large fireplace kept the room illuminated with a nice warm glow.

Santa and Mrs. Claus would sit at one end of their large dining room table. And what a splendid table it was! A long solid wood table, able to seat two dozen people, with little happy faces carved on the sides. The back of each chair was also carved with little happy faces with red velvet seat cushions. Santa always said, "I only want to see happy faces around the dinner table, even if every chair is not always filled."

In the past Santa and Mrs. Claus had discussed what to do about the barns being filled with toys. Now it was happening every night and finally, one night at dinner they found a solution.

Mrs. Claus reminded Santa, "Our friends have suggested we sell the toys. They could produce a nice income."

"No" Santa exclaimed, "I did not make all those toys to sell. Each one has a part of me in it and is carved and painted with love."

Mrs. Claus knew that was true. Every time she brought in a cookie or a piece of pie while Santa was working on a toy, she could see in his eyes the love of what he was doing.

"Besides," he continued, "there are not many people in this part of the country who can afford to spend their money on toys."

This was also true. Most of the people in the North Forest region made enough money for their own needs but did not have enough for extras. And, toys would be an extra expense.

They especially would not be able to afford the price of Santa's toys. Each toy was handmade, taking many hours to make. They were sturdy, and painted perfectly. The face on each doll showed remarkable expression. The wheels on each wagon were carved perfectly round. The rocking horses rocked back-and-forth very smoothly without any wiggling or bumping and the baby carriages had fine spindled wheels.

Santa took great pride in the perfection put into every toy. "Do we need the money?" he asked, taking a sip of his hot chocolate. "Are you getting tired of this lifestyle?" He asked with a sad, hurt tone in his voice.

"Oh no," she replied. "You know that I would live anywhere as long as I was with you." She came around to his end of the table, filled his hot chocolate mug, and then gave him a big kiss on his rosy cheek. She set the hot chocolate kettle on its rack by the fire and sat back down. They both sat quietly for a few minutes and watched the fire. It was pleasant to feel the heat of the fire coming from the large stone fireplace. The burning logs filled the large dining room with a warm flickering glow. It had been snowing most of the day. In the evening dusk, the wind could be heard outside, swaying the snow laden branches high above the roof. This made the dining room all that much more warm and cozy.

Finally Mrs. Claus asked in a quiet voice, "What is the purpose of your toys?" Santa looked away from the fire and at her and asked, "What do you mean?" She reached over and laid her hand on top of his hand and asked "What is the purpose of your toys or for that matter, any toy?" Santa answered, "To make people happy, to make children happy! Children need something to play with. They made me happy just working on them, designing them and painting them."

"Do you think those toys are making anyone happy stacked in our barns?" She asked quietly.

"I am not going to sell the toys!" Santa grumped. "That was not the reason I made them" his voice getting a little bit louder, slightly annoyed.

"Now, now." Mrs. Claus answered, patting his hand. "I was not suggesting you sell your toys." She grabbed his hand in both of hers and gave a little squeeze and said, "I think you should GIVE your toys away." Well that certainly made the figgleberry pudding in his tummy wiggle around! "Give the toys away? Give the toys away?" Santa almost choked on his hot chocolate. "Mama," said Santa, his pet name for Mrs. Claus, "I do not understand how you could suggest that! After all the love and care I put into making those toys, you suggest I give them away?" Obviously, this thought had never occurred to Santa.

Fortunately, Mrs. Claus had many years of experience in anticipating Santa's thoughts. She had a compelling answer ready. "Have you ever seen the children's wide opened eyes when they go into the barns?" The children she referred to were their workers' children. The twelve children had full run of the farm, often helping their fathers with the chores.

"I sure do", Santa replied, "They would love to get their hands on some of those toys."

Mrs. Claus continued with a little twinkle in her voice, "Can you imagine what joy they would have if they could have those toys and play with them? Can you imagine the joy any child would have if they received a toy such as yours as a gift?"

Santa finished his hot chocolate in three big gulps and set his mug down on the table. He leaned forward clasping his hands together and stared into the fire. Mrs. Claus got up, pulled the hot chocolate kettle off its rack and quietly refilled Santa's mug. After returning the kettle to the rack, she removed three large marshmallows from a bowl at her center of the table and plunked them into his hot chocolate.

"Give the toys away," Santa said quietly to himself as he sat deep in thought.

After a few moments Mrs. Claus asked in a quiet voice, "Imagine if you can, a little girl waking up on one of these cold winter mornings and finding a beautiful doll wrapped up in a blanket on her front doorstep. Or imagine a young boy finding one of your red wagons on his front doorstep. The happiness you would have provided those children would make the building of the next toy so much more fun for you."?

For a long while, Santa slowly rocked back and forth in his chair, thinking. Mrs. Claus sat quietly by, humming softly while sewing, filling his mug with hot chocolate and marshmallows two more times. They both sat quietly, listening to the crackling of the fire.

Finally, he sat up straight, put both hands face down on the table, puffed out his chest and said, "Mama, I think I have come up with a solution. I am going to give the toys away. There are kids that would enjoy my toys and they can provide many years of happiness." He sat there with a very proud look on his face.

Mrs. Claus replied, "I think that is a splendid idea, I am glad you thought of it." She then got up, poured him another mug of hot cocoa and started clearing the dishes from the table. Life was in good order.

However, this decision is what started the challenges for Santa and Mrs. Claus. But before we go into that, there is one very important topic that should be discussed. That is the topic of Santa's success.

SANTA'S MAGIC

There is no record of how Santa became prosperous or the source of his income. But we know that he owned a very large homestead with many large barns and buildings used to store the crops from the farm year after year. Santa was generous with everyone around him. He was a great friend and neighbor to all, even helping families from other towns; many were people he had never even met. He was always able to pay his workers well and for the materials and paints for making toys. Mrs. Claus's flour bins and sugar cans were always well stocked. How was that possible?

This leads us to wonder how and when Santa might have used magic powers. Santa's jolly nature could be deemed as magical. He had the knack of making people around him feel happy. His robust "Ho Ho Ho's" always brought smiles to people's faces. His presence seemed to have a magical effect on everybody surrounding him. Everyone was Santa's friend.

Santa's magical powers seemed to be fascinating. There were many occasions when he was able to perform activities that appeared to be beyond possible. Quite often he would be asked, "How did you do that?" He often answers with a twinkle in his eye, "I used my magic." The many references about magic and Santa Claus started very early in his life. Evidence of magical powers is apparent throughout the story of Santa and the North Pole. The world should feel fortunate those powers landed in the hands of a person with a good heart and character, not someone who was evil or selfish. All who knew him, considered Santa Claus to be a good man. How he obtained magical powers has yet to be discovered, but evidently he had them.

SANTA'S TOYS

The very next day after Santa came up with his wonderful idea of giving his toys away, (now we know it was Mrs. Claus's idea) he couldn't wait to gather the children together. At the first signs of daylight, he jumped out of bed and dressed as fast as possible. He ran down stairs, where he could hear Mrs. Claus clinking pots and pans, preparing breakfast. He sat down at his place at the kitchen table. He immediately gulped down a large cup of hot chocolate. He ate his eggs almost as fast as Mrs. Claus put them on his plate. He finished his eggs before she could put the first stack of pancakes on his plate.

Mrs. Claus's kitchen was always warm and toasty. It always had a hustle and bustle atmosphere that included Mrs. Claus and usually one or two of the worker's wives preparing the daily meals. On days when there was no school, one or two of the children might be helping in the kitchen as well. It was always a fun place for them to help with the chores. They got to lick the spoons and clean out the candy bowls on the days Mrs. Claus made candy. Every one of the children loved the opportunity to help in the kitchen. Mrs. Claus's friendly nature made them all feel welcome. She always made sure the candy mixing bowls and spoons were well worth licking.

"Whoa, whoa," Mrs. Claus exclaimed as she watched Santa gobble down a stack of pancakes almost instantly. "Why are you in such a hurry?" She asked. She knew the animals had already been fed and there was not a lot that could be done this time of year when there was three feet of snow on the ground. The men would be in one of the barns today, repairing tools and farm equipment. There were no projects that needed to be done with any great urgency.

"I want to see if the children would be interested in some of the toys." When he said this, Cven, age ten and Henri, aged nine, who were helping in the kitchen whirled around and looked at Santa with eyes wide open. Both were thinking…be interested in some of his toys? Do you think they would have wanted some of Santa's toys?

"Cven, Henri, please run and tell the rest of the children to meet here as quickly as possible."

They were out the door quicker than a whistle. Although the snow was almost up to their knees, the boys got to each of the farm houses very quickly.

"What are you doing?" Mildred asked Santa, as she was peeling potatoes. "I want to see if the children would be interested in any of my toys." Santa replied while still gobbling down his second large stack of pancakes.

"You must be joking," Mildred said, "it takes all our energy each day to keep the children away from your toys."

"I know, and I am deeply sorry for not even thinking about that. They are all good kids and there is absolutely no reason why they shouldn't have been able to play with these toys all these years, instead of just looking at them." Both Mildred and Sarah glanced over at Mrs. Claus. She just smiled and winked. There had been many discussions in the kitchen about how difficult it was to keep the children away from Santa's toys. This is one of the unusual aspects of Santa's history. He had always been very generous with the people around him. Why he never thought of offering the children of his farm families some of his toys is a question that has mystified the experts for ages. We can only guess that he was so captivated with the making and painting of so many unique toys, he gave no thought of them being objects for play.

Over the next few minutes the kitchen door opened and closed many times as the children came bustling in. They had run down the snow covered lane to the Clauses' kitchen. Each was handed a big cup of hot chocolate as they came through the door. They stomped the snow off their feet before sliding over in front of one of the kitchen fires. Their faces, rosy from the cold outside, had wide-eyed looks and grins of anticipation as they all said good morning to Santa and Mrs. Claus. The fact is they were all waiting to hear whether or not the news about the toys was true. Santa was wiping his mustache after finishing his third stack of pancakes.

He laid his napkin down on the table, stood up and said "Children, will you follow me out to the barn? I have something I want to ask you." They all nodded their heads vigorously. Charlotte, a cute little five-year-old girl, clapped her hands with glee, hardly able to contain herself. "Follow me," Santa commanded, leading a dozen bouncing children through the house and out the front door.

The biggest barn was right across the yard. The earthen ramp led up to two big sliding doors. Santa undid the latch and slid one door open. One of the older boys helped Santa and slid the other door open. The children did not usually have any reason for going into this particular barn. It was mostly used for parking wagons and sleighs. This involved the men tethering the large workhorses, securing them and the wagons inside the barn, a process that was not safe for the children to be around. As the doors slid open, the sunlight reflecting off the white snow, lit up the inside of the barn. The

children gasped! Stacked all around the edges of the barn where heaps and piles of wonderfully carved and painted toys, much the same as they had seen in the other barns. But this barn was enormous, making the piles of toys all the more enticing, as their eyes followed from one wall to the other, wagons, wooden horses, dolls and carriages, games, playhouses, toys beyond all imagination sat just waiting for their owner. Toys were hanging everywhere showing off a wonderland of color and amazement.

"Would you like any of these toys?" Santa asked. They all turned toward him with wide eyes and mouths gaped open. They just could not believe what they were hearing! Could it be true!

"Oh, Santa, that would be wonderful," One of them exclaimed.

"Alright, it is time for each one of you to choose a toy for yourself," He commanded.

"Yahoo!" they shouted, scattering through the wagons and sleighs to get to the stacks of toys. There was laughter and great joy as each child brought a toy to the open area by the barn doors. The crisp cold air of the morning had no effect on the children. They were just giddy with delight! Santa was overwhelmed watching the joy on the faces of these children. He never felt so exhilarated in his whole life, as he experienced great delight watching how happy he had made the children.

"Okay," he said when all the children were back in front of him, each with a toy. "Now put those toys down". Instantly there was a look of horror on each child's face. But in the next instant, Santa shouted "... and go get another one!" The children squealed with delight, laying their toys carefully on the barn floor and scurrying through the barn picking through the heaps and piles of toys, each one grabbing another toy. By this time, their parents and Mrs. Claus had come out from where they were working and gathered at the front door of the barn. What commotion!

"Such uproar, what is going on here?" one of them asked.

"Santa is giving some of his toys to the children," answered Mrs. Claus who had now moved to Santa's side at the open barn doors. The children excitedly showed their parents the toys they had carefully chosen. Each of them ran up and gave Santa a big hug. Each of the mothers came over to Santa, gave him a hug and a thank you. The whole event was filled with great excitement and joy.

Although the sun was out, a brisk northern breeze was blowing, whipping up gusts of swirling snow, making the temperatures seem much colder.

"Everybody in the house for hot chocolate and pudding," Mrs. Claus ordered in her sweet voice, over the hubbub of excited voices. With the children, still showing their parents their wonderful gifts, they all trudged through the snow toward the front door of the Clauses' house. Santa and Mrs. Claus trailed behind.

"You are a wonderful man," Mrs. Claus said quietly to her husband as they walked toward the front door hand in hand.

"Mama," replied Santa, "this has been one of the best days of my life. Except for the day I married you of course" he looked down at her with a twinkle in his eye.

The rest of the day was spent in the big dining room. Fortunately, the big dining table could seat well over two dozen people. The children played gleefully in front of the fireplace with their new toys. The ladies talked among themselves. The men talked about how well the previous crop season had been. They discussed whether a new barn needed to be built due to the lack of space caused by the toys. Santa told them how the toy problem was going to be resolved. Eventually, the men returned to the workbenches where they had been working earlier that day. Santa went with them, to get away from the constant noise of the excited children, smiling as he heard the laughter from behind.

The merriment continued through the evening. Eventually each family walked briskly back down the lanes to their homes, wrapped warmly as they went out the front door. The cold December night was certainly going to put a rosy glow on everybody's cheeks before they were home.

Later, as they were preparing for bed, Santa said, "This has been a wonderful day."

"You have done a wonderful thing today," Mrs. Claus replied, as she getting under the covers.

"I think tomorrow I will ask the older children to do a task for me." Santa said."What is that?" Mrs. Claus inquired.

"I would like the names of all the children here in the North Forest," Santa replied.

The North Forest area was a very large area. It extended many miles in each direction from the Clauses' Farm. The region was mostly forest with huge trees like those that surrounded the Clauses' home. Cleared farmland was present, growing enough food for families that tended their farm. Families lived great distances from each other. However, the children would know most of the other children in the region through the school.

"And why do you want all their names?" Mrs. Claus asked, already knowing the answer.

"Did you see the looks in the children's faces today?" Santa inquired, "There is nothing more wonderful than seeing the joy on children's faces. I get great joy from making toys. However, that joy does not compare to the joy I feel when I see how happy a toy makes a child," Santa said, as he was blowing out the last candle in their bedroom. He then slid under the covers and pulled them up to his neck. Unfortunately, we cannot answer the most often asked question about Santa. We do not know whether Santa put his beard outside the covers or under the covers!

Mrs. Claus

As we mentioned earlier, the good nature of the Clauses is what created their problems. Santa had an easy-going, very likable nature. But as the years went by, maintaining his good nature was probably due to Mrs. Claus's easy going personality. She had a very good calming effect on Santa and everyone else around her. There are no records telling how Santa and Mrs. Claus met or even when they got married. However, it was obvious to everyone they were very much in love. Each of them seemed to make it their primary responsibility to take care of the other. That is a wonderful present for all married couples today.

It was very rare to hear Mrs. Claus make a negative comment about any situation or any person. On occasion she could be heard scolding Santa. This occurred more often after they moved to the North Pole as Christmas approached each year. As the pressure builds at the approach of Christmas Eve, often the commotion of activity at the North Pole would be overwhelming. Occasionally you could hear her scolding Santa, but not too harsh, mostly to get him to concentrate on the time schedule. Fortunately, Santa never let it affect him because he knew she was doing it for everyone's benefit. She was good at taking care of details. Whether preparing a large dinner for guests or making sure Santa kept to his schedules, she was the one who usually kept things organized and moving in the right direction in an orderly fashion.

Always, she has been a wise and trustworthy companion for Santa. When things seemed out of control, she brought calm. She always found the positive in any situation. She never criticized. Mrs. Claus never chastised anyone for their mistakes. She felt life was too short to make anybody feel bad about something they did wrong. It was better that they learned from their mistakes so they could do better the next time. She was very good at resolving problems. Everybody loved Mrs. Claus. She knew how to cook and sew, too. She had the ability to hand someone a cup of hot cocoa at just the right time to change what might have been an ugly situation. The women on the farm loved to work with her in the kitchen. Not only did they learn how to prepare scrumptious meals, they also received sage advice on family life. Mrs. Claus shared her wisdom gracefully.

Mrs. Claus makes all her clothes and Santa's too. Her dresses usually were floor length. She said this helped to keep her toes warm. Her beautiful long white flowing hair was usually wrapped as a bun on the top of her head. Santa adored her button nose. And her cheeks were always rosy. Her wire rim glasses usually slid way down on her nose while she was sewing and working in the kitchen. She is the perfect image of everybody's grandmother.

Christmas Night

As mentioned earlier, the good nature and generosity of the Clauses is what eventually created a problem. Once Santa saw the joy when his toys were given to the children, all he could think about was how was he going to make the process even bigger? He had the children at the farm provide him with a list of names of all the children in the North Forest region. It was a long list. Santa spent many nights studying the ages of the boys and girls on the list.

Finally, at dinner one night he made an announcement to Mrs. Claus. "Mama, I am going to give my toys to all the children in the North Forest."

"How do you plan on doing that?" She asked as she was filling Santa's bowl with another scoop of stew. "I am not sure yet," he answered as he picked up his spoon and continued eating. "But I think I have a plan."

"Tell me your plan," Mrs. Claus requested as she was settling back into her chair.

Santa placed his spoon on the table and took a big swallow of his hot chocolate. "This is what I have been thinking. Although it would be well accepted by many in the North Forest for gifts to be given to their children, the folks up here are a very hard working, proud people. There are probably some who might take offense to being given gifts for the children without being able to repay." Mrs. Claus nodded in an understanding manner. "I think I will deliver presents to each family at night in the cover of darkness. That way, parents will not have to be confronted." Mrs. Claus continued to nod approvingly.

"How do you plan to deliver all the toys? You are not thinking you can do it all in one night, are you?" asked Mrs. Claus. Although the North Forest was not heavily populated, the habitants lived many miles apart. Delivering to every house in the region would require many hundreds of miles of travel.

"I think I can get all the toys loaded into our four big wagons," Santa answered as he got up and placed another log on the fire. "I will have the men drive the wagons. With a little bit of magic, I am pretty sure we could get all the toys delivered in one night." he said, as he winked at Mrs. Claus.

"When do you propose to make this trek into the night?" Mrs. Claus inquired, knowing that logically a project such as this could not possibly be done in one night, but if Santa said he could do it, he probably would be able to do it.

"That I am not sure," replied Santa, "but it should be soon. Late December is always the darkest and dreariest time of the year. What better time to bring some happiness to the children?" He was now tapping his pipe and getting ready for a nice after dinner smoke.

"Why not do it on the Holy night, December 25th? What better night for promoting the lesson of giving? That is only four more days away." she suggested.

"What a good idea!" replied Santa. The rest of the evening was spent discussing all the details required for making such a trip. The horses needed to be well fed. Mrs. Claus would be sure the men would have big pots of hot apple cider stored underneath their seats. All of the wagons would need the ski runners since heavy snow falls of the past week had left several more feet of snow on the ground.

She could hear the excitement building in Santa's voice as he discussed all the details of the coming venture. They talked and made plans until bedtime.

THE SUNRISE RETURN

As can be imagined, Mrs. Claus did not sleep very well that night. More than likely, none of the women on Santa's farm slept soundly. When Mrs. Claus arose and went down to the kitchen to start breakfast, it was still dark outside. She glanced out the window to see if there were any signs of the wagons. All she could see was darkness. After the fires were stoked to make them warmer, and the hot chocolate was started on the stove, a knock was heard on the kitchen door as Mildred and Sarah let themselves in. They quickly removed their coats, hung them up and stood close to the fire to get warm. They told Mrs. Claus they had seen none of the wagons as they were came up the lane toward her kitchen.

"They will be all right," she assured them. "Santa would not let anything happen to any of them." This comforted the women. They went to work as normal, cracking open eggs and stirring up pancake batter.

It was with the first slight ray of daylight when the familiar "Ho Ho Ho!" could be heard in the distance. The women all ran to the window. As the wagons slid through the snow past the other houses, they could see the children running out to meet Santa and their fathers. Some of them ran along beside the wagons. The others were hauled up by their fathers to sit next to them on the seat while they continued up the lane toward the house. The women scurried back to preparing the breakfast, knowing that everyone would be hungry after a long cold night trekking through the North Forest. "Ho Ho Ho!" the familiar laughter rang out again and again as the wagons proceeded toward the house. The comforting sound of the wagon bells could be heard getting louder and louder. As they pulled into the yard, Santa jumped off his wagon into the deep snow and practically bounded up the front steps. Mrs. Claus met him at the front door and they gave each other a big hug.

"Cven," she called toward the wagons as they were being moved into the barn, "come in and build up the fire." Cven jumped off the back of the wagon his father was driving and had to take high steps to get through the snow to the front porch.

33

Turning back to Santa, Mrs. Claus begged, "Please tell us what happened, how everything went!" as she helped remove his big heavy winter coat, hat, and scarf.

"In time Mama, the men are starving. They will be in as soon as they take care of the horses." He gave her a friendly kiss on the nose and she headed back toward the kitchen. He walked into the dining room and helped Cven put logs on the fire.

Soon the men came in the front door and each was met with a big hug from their wives. They were helped in getting their heavy coats, gloves, hats and scarves off and hung up to dry. The dining room once again became a frenzy of excited talking and laughter. The women brought in platters piled high with eggs, bacon, biscuits and gravy, butter, syrup and pancakes for the hungry group. Although they were tired from their all-night expedition, everyone was talking excitedly as they ate. Everyone was asking questions. The children wanted to know if it was scary being in the dark all night while others asked if they had run into any problems. The hullabaloo in the dining room remained constant with questioning.

"Hold on, hold on," Santa bellowed, trying to be heard over all the conversation. "Let us finish our breakfast. Then we will tell you everything that happened." Everybody quieted down. The children climbed into chairs and helped consume all the eggs and pancakes.

After everyone had eaten until full, the table was cleared. Everybody's mugs were filled with hot chocolate and marshmallows.

As the women sat down, Mrs. Claus said to Santa, "Okay, tell us everything that happened. Did you run into problems, did you get to everyone? Were the gifts accepted? Did you run into any danger? How did you…."

At that point, Santa threw up his hands and exclaimed "Whoa Mama, one question at a time. The men and I are tired but we had a fun night filled with exhilaration! We will tell you everything that happened, as it will take a good while to warm our bones next to the fire." He winked at her with that twinkle in his eye. He looked around the table and then asked the men, "Do you want me to do the talking or do you want to tell about the evening?"

"Oh no, you give the details Santa. We will fill in as you go along." They all nodded their heads in agreement.

Santa's Description of Christmas Night

"Okay," Santa started, "as we all know, once it gets dark in the North Forest, it is really dark. Fortunately, the fresh snow made the forest lanes just barely distinguishable. The glow of our lanterns was often the only light that could be seen in any direction. The horses have a good sense of where to go and for that we were thankful. We delivered toys starting with the closest families. This lightened the load for the horses. At most of the houses we were able to deliver the toys without anyone knowing we were there! The heavy snow muffled our sound significantly, making four large wagons and teams very quiet as we slid past many very secluded homes."

"Did anyone see you or talk with you?" interrupted Mrs. Claus.

"Certainly Mama, we ran into a number of adults as we were placing toys by the front doors." Santa said as he tapped his knife, getting it ready for another wood carving, most likely wheels for another toy.

Santa continued "As a matter of fact, we have some plucked turkeys and chickens in the wagons. There were some folks who insisted we take something as their gift. I assured them there was absolutely no reason they had to give us anything, the toys were gifts for the children, but they insisted. There were others who felt uncomfortable that they could not give something back in return. I made it very clear to them that it was unnecessary. I shared with them that there is no better feeling in the world than giving to others, and to give there must be someone to receive."

The men nodded in agreement as they sat around the fireplace. The children sat in silence listening to every word from Santa.

"Did you run into any trouble?" Mildred asked.

"Not real trouble," Santa replied, "but we did have a few close calls!" "We sure did," piped in Adam, the thoughtful one of Santa's workers. He was the one who usually found the solutions for problems on the farm. "Especially that fellow we ran into down by Pikesville." He continued.

"Ah yes," Santa interjected quickly, seeing the glare coming from Mrs. Claus. "Fortunately, that turned out all right."

"We are waiting to hear the details," Mrs. Claus stated as she impatiently tapped her toes on the floor. All the children looked at her. They had never heard a disparaging tone of voice from her ever.

"Oh, yes that was a close one." Santa continued. "Old man Hanson came barreling out of the bushes as we approached his house. He had his blunderbuss primed and loaded." A blunderbuss is a very large gun people used to protect themselves from wild animals in the old days. "What are you doing sneaking around here at night?" Old man Hanson yelled. "I almost shot you. What are you doing? Are you out looting?"

"I had to quickly calm him down." Santa continued, "I told him I was delivering toys for his children. He looked at all of us as if we were kind of crazy. He asked us if we had been drinking too much giggleberry juice! He could not imagine anyone out in the middle of the night --- delivering toys! He finally settled down, we left the toys, but he watched us every inch of the way until we were completely out of sight." The men around the table smiled and chuckled as they listened to Santa's description of the situation.

"Then there was the fella who almost shot you off the wagon because he thought you were a bull moose coming up the lane." Adam piped in again. Mrs. Claus put her hand to her mouth in a horrified expression.

"Yessirree, that was a close one also." Santa exclaimed glancing at Adam with a look that said keep your mouth shut.

"Ho Ho Ho!" Santa laughed, "He said my big furry coat made me look like a big animal. But didn't we have a wonderful time? There are hundreds of children waking up this morning finding gifts at their front door. I wish we could all be there to see their faces." The men again nodded in agreement.

Sarah, Adam's wife, also was good at solving problems. But tonight's travels did not add up. "I am not understanding something," she inquired, "The horses pull the wagons at two miles per hour. You delivered toys to hundreds of families across the North Forest. That was hundreds and hundreds of miles of traveling. How did you get to everyone in just over twelve hours? How is that possible?"

Eric, the eldest of the farmhands replied, "I was wondering that myself, but as we were traveling and delivering, time seemed to come to a standstill. We didn't really notice it at the time. It seemed like we were doing many things and time was hardly passing." The other farmhands voiced their agreement. They turned their attention back to Santa.

Sarah asked, "Santa, do you have an explanation?"

"I think so," Santa replied. "What were the feelings you were having as we delivered the toys, imagining how the children would be reacting when they found them in the morning?" He looked at each of his farmhands. "Exhilarated, euphoric, a sense of love and joy they had never felt before" were the answers.

Santa continued, "I think it must be the excitement of the night that makes us able to do things at much faster speeds than we think we are moving. I also felt invigorated beyond anything I have ever felt before this past evening. It felt like there was magic in the air." He winked at Mrs. Claus with that twinkle in his eye.

Everyone around the table, while they didn't fully understand Santa's explanation, accepted it. It should be noted that this is again another instance where something that seemed impossible could be accomplished by Santa Claus. Do not dismiss the power his magic may have!

The conversation in the dining room continued for another hour, everyone telling stories and experiences that occurred through the wee hours of the night. They also discussed that some space had been cleared from the barns but not nearly enough. They wondered if there would be enough room for the next harvest.

"If not," said Santa, "we will just have to do this again." They all laughed heartily at the thought. It was a unique experience but not likely to have the same effect in the future. Soon, the fatigue started catching up to them. After a nice big breakfast, hot chocolates, and getting warmed up next to the large fireplace, the men began to sag. They donned their coats and hats and wandered back to their houses. All of them, even Santa, went to bed about noon time and slept soundly until the next morning.

The day was over for them. But the news of the evening's activities ran throughout the North Forest area like a wildfire. The next day, many families, when attending their worship services, compared stories about the wonderful gifts they had found on their doorsteps that morning. Santa was not looking for any grand acknowledgment for his nighttime excursion. He did it because he felt in his heart that giving was a good thing. But the result would be overwhelming. Toys for the children! Parents who could never afford toys for their children became forever grateful for someone else's thoughtfulness. It took very little time for everyone in the North Forest to realize they had received gifts from Santa Claus. The stories grew larger.

The legend grew larger. It was rumored that Santa must have an army to deliver that many toys in one night. Many pondered why he did it. His good reputation blossomed many-fold throughout the North Forest and beyond. As we all know, it did not end there. Each year his list of children grew longer and longer. He would make toys all year long to be delivered throughout the region in one night. Everyone loved receiving toys from Santa Claus.

Santa's Decision to Move North

Throughout the region, the more widespread his name was known, the more beloved he became. His many visitors throughout the year would keep him informed of how his generosity was greatly appreciated by many people who did not even know him. Unfortunately, this great popularity made things difficult for Santa and Mrs. Claus to continue to live on their lovely North Forest farm. You see, most of the ruling class at that time ruled because they were royalty. This royalty was passed from one generation to the next. You did not have to be a good ruler or a popular ruler. Your birthright was what gave you the power to rule over the area's inhabitants. They were becoming very uncomfortable and perhaps a little jealous over this person called Santa Claus in the North Forest who had the admiration of the whole country side. They heard he had armies of followers helping to deliver tokens of appreciation each December. They heard he must have had mystical powers. He could do things that most people believed to be impossible. As Santa's reputation grew, so did the subtle threats by the ruling class towards him and Mrs. Claus. After a few years, the effects of those threats could be seen. Mrs. Claus was not her cheerful self anymore. She had trouble sleeping at night. She did not feel like baking pies or making candy anymore. The cheerfulness had left the once big, friendly happy home of the Clauses.

"Mama," Santa said to her one morning as she was working lethargically in the kitchen, "I think it is time we move away from this area." She looked up at him with sad eyes but a faint look of relief. For the past few years, she had been greatly worried about Santa when he was away from the farm. She did not know what the royalty might do to him. She feared they could kidnap him and she might not ever hear from him again. They might come and destroy their beautiful home in North Forest. All these concerns had been weighing upon her for many months.

"Where would we go," she asked looking up at her husband whom she loved so very much. "How can we leave our beautiful home?"

Santa gave her a big warm hug. "Don't worry, as long as we have each other we will always have a happy home, no matter where we are." Then they both remembered what they heard as a child, "Home is where you hang your hat."

That is how the Clauses first began their search for a safe place to make toys and candy. Santa knew he would have to search for territory that was further north where the tentacles of the ruling class would not be able to reach out and put a damper on their lives. Once the decision was made to move, Mrs. Claus became her old self again, exuding confidence and the positive outlook for which she was so well known. There were many details that would have to be taken care of before they started north. However, she was greatly relieved; knowing the safety of her husband and friends was the most important result from this move.

HEADING FOR THE NORTH POLE

The four large wagons and three smaller wagons were packed and piled high with furniture, cooking utensils, large supplies of sugar, cinnamon, flour and Santa's work tools. The horses were all tethered to the wagons, standing patiently as the last supplies were being stowed under the drivers' seats. The wagons were gathered in the yard, in front of the house like they had been five years ago, for that unforgettable night that started the Christmas tradition. There were now 18 children standing on the front porch. All had tears in their eyes as they gave Santa and Mrs. Claus their goodbye hugs. The women brought out food to put underneath the seats, knowing their husbands may not be back for a few weeks. They each embraced Santa and Mrs. Claus with tears.

The past few weeks had been a frenzy of activity. The furniture that could be packed had to be carefully put in the wagons. Many pieces of furniture were too big to take with them. The dining room table and chairs with the many happy faces carved into them had to be left behind. Santa assured Mrs. Claus that wherever they were going, they would find people who could make them new furniture.

Santa had worked out very fair arrangements for the workers to take over the farm. He gave Adam the responsibility for the farm operations. This was agreeable with the other families. A portion of the funds were to be sent to Santa and Mrs. Claus while the remaining portion would be shared with each family. It was decided that Adam and Sarah and their children would move in to the Clauses' house. The house left by Adam and Sarah would be available for any new family additions.

There were many tears in the group as they helped Mrs. Claus climb up onto the seat of the first wagon. The women continued to hand her last-minute presents, such as quilts and pillows, to make her ride on the wagon more comfortable. The men all climbed up on their wagons, the older boys, who were now teenagers, would be driving the smaller wagons. Sobs could be heard from the group of women and children standing on the porch as Santa snapped the reins of the lead wagon. Tears trickled down Mrs. Claus's cheeks as she raised a hand and waved goodbye. Saying goodbye to people we care about can be very difficult but we can carry the wonderful memory of them with us forever.

The caravan of wagons slowly circled around the front yard area, the drivers waving to their wives and children. As the line of wagons started slowly rumbling down the lane, Mrs. Claus gazed back with tears in her eyes for a last look at her home that had so many years of happy memories. Sitting next to her husband, she waved to all, as they pulled out of sight. When she could see the house no more, she turned back around and slid her arm under her husband's arm and looked forward, anticipating what the future might bring, after all they had each other.

Traveling North

The traveling was slow as the heavy-laden wagons lumbered along the rugged roads. The weather had the first tinges of autumn in the air. Santa had wanted to leave earlier in the year but knew the men could not be spared until all the crops were harvested and put in the now empty barns since most of the toys had been delivered over the past few years. The first few days of travel were especially hard for Mrs. Claus. Her heart was heavy with sadness as she reminisced about all the pleasant years of gaiety they had experienced in their home in the North Forest. Santa kept reassuring her that wherever they were going they would make their new home just as warm and welcoming. She tried not to show her concern, holding tightly onto his arm as they rode together. "Yes," she would say, "everything is going to be just fine." Her sadness and doubts slowly disappeared the further north they traveled. They spent their nights at inns, eating good hearty meals after their long days of traveling.

Of course, Santa's jolly nature enlivened the dining halls. His talent for telling stories, punctuated with his hearty "Ho Ho Ho's" became the source of merriment to all those in earshot. He kept everybody entertained well into the evening. Each morning the ritual was the same. After a hearty breakfast and hitching of the teams, all the overnight guests would say their farewells with hearty handshakes as though they all had been friends for many years. Meeting and enjoying new people refreshed the spirits of Mrs. Claus. She knew wherever their new home would be, they would have many friends. As they pulled away, Santa would wave goodbye and he was so memorable in his big red suit.

Oh yes, before we go any further, Santa was adorned in his now well-known red suit. As you may recall, the fact that Santa had almost been shot with blunderbusses, because he was mistaken as a big furry animal, had not gone unnoticed by Mrs. Claus. She had been horrified that Santa had been mistaken for a bull Moose, although she did not think too much about it until it became evident that Santa was going to do another toy delivery the following December 25th. She gathered all the women and older girls together in their great dining hall. The project was to make a warm outfit for Santa to keep him from being a mistaken target! After throwing many ideas back-and-forth, the consensus was to design a suit that would clearly show no resemblance to a wild animal. The color red was chosen. It was soon embellished with white furry trim at the end of the sleeves and the bottom of the coat. Bright black buttons and a nice shiny black belt were added as highlights. A red cap with white fur lining was designed to keep Santa's head warm.

The evening of Santa's second all night trek the ladies presented Santa with his new outfit. He immediately went upstairs and put it on. Coming back downstairs in his new apparel, he looked prouder than a peacock. As he modeled his new red suit, everyone admired him with oohs and aah's. "Why have I deserved the honor of such a fine outfit?" Santa asked with much humor in his voice.

"Because I did not want you hanging in someone's meat barn mistaken for a Bull Moose animal," replied Mrs. Claus.

With that Santa leaned back, put his hands on his stomach and let out a loud "Ho Ho Ho!" stating that was one of the funniest things he had ever heard. Since that time, Mrs. Claus made sure Santa had a good supply of his fancy red outfits. Needless to say, no one else had such a distinct work outfit as Santa's.

Each day the caravan of wagons continued their journey northward. The days began to turn dark earlier; the autumn temperatures dropped the further north they traveled. Mrs. Claus was concerned about finding a new home before hard winter weather set in. She also wondered how Santa was going to be able to make enough toys before December 25th, if he was planning on delivering again that year. He assured her the toys would be ready. Each year, his list of children grew as more and more people learned about his activities.

The caravan of wagons rolled slowly through the heavily wooded forests, each wagon creaking softly as the heavy wheels rolled along the North Forest dirt roads. The tall pine trees swayed softly high overhead in the breeze. Birds could be heard chirping as they flitted back and forth across the caravan's path. Occasionally a few deer and elk could be spotted through the trees, silently moving away into the forest as the wagons rolled past. In many areas, the tree cover was so thick, only occasional rays of sunlight could reach the ground. In the early stages of the journey, the Clauses saw small farmhouses and log cabins and were greeted by the families as they slowly lumbered past or occasionally stopped to water the horses. The further north they traveled, the fewer houses they saw, and soon they were traveling where almost no homes existed.

The temperature had become considerably colder. Each day at the end of many hours of travel, Santa, Mrs. Claus, and the other men and boys were very grateful as they approached a friendly inn. At each inn, Santa would inquire about the distance to the next inn. After a few weeks

of travel when he was informed that the next inn would be the last one, he knew he was getting very close to the northernmost areas of the world. He knew there were very few people who lived in this region; however, his major concern was to make sure Mrs. Claus did not feel threatened by the power of the royalty, no matter in what part of the world they decided to live. Although the weather continued to get much colder and the daylight hours much shorter, the Clauses felt more relieved the more they left civilization behind.

It was dark when they finally reached the last inn. The Elfinland Inn was a big majestic inn, unexpected for such a sparsely populated area! However, it was the only inn for many miles around as there were not many other places to go. It was dusk when the small caravan of wagons approached the inn. The wagons lumbered into the large courtyard area. Santa pulled his lead wagon up to the front steps and helped Mrs. Claus step down from her seat. While the men took the wagons to the back to unhitch the teams to lead them into the stables, Santa and Mrs. Claus climbed the steps onto the porch, a wide veranda that surrounded the entire front of the inn. Opening the large front doors, they stepped into a warm, welcoming room. Two large fireplaces were ablaze with big, healthy, crackling fires. From behind the registration counter, a giant of a man welcomed them. He stretched out his big meaty hand to Santa and flashed a friendly grin from behind his big red beard and mustache. "Welcome to the Elfinland Inn. My name is Ivan. I hope we can make your stay very pleasant."

Santa shook his hand. "Thank you, we have had a long journey to get to this part of the world." After they registered for rooms for themselves and the men, Ivan motioned them toward the dining area. "Come, sit, have some hot cider to warm you up."

"Thank you very much," replied Santa, "however, do you happen to have hot chocolate?" As they journeyed north, most of the inns served hot cider but none had the cinnamon sticks that Mrs. Claus used. Their hot cider was good but not as good as what Mrs. Claus made.

"We certainly do!" Ivan replied. "Ingrid," he yelled through a kitchen doorway, "bring us a large pot of hot cocoa." Ivan motioned them to a big table near one of the fireplaces. He sat down and joined them. Soon the table filled up as the men came in. There were a small number of guests sitting at other tables in the large dining area. As so often happened, Santa's gregarious and jolly nature, complemented by Ivan's good spirited personality, filled the room with good-natured entertainment. Ingrid, Ivan's wife and Eva, his daughter, served the travelers hot chocolate and a big hearty meal. They too, sat and enjoyed the festive atmosphere.

As the evening wore on, Ivan inquired, "Where are you folks going?" "We would like to settle down in this area." replied Santa.

This brought a look of surprise on Ivan's face. "That surprises me," said Ivan. "Not many people want to settle this far North. What type of work do you do?"

"I am involved with making toys," said Santa, as he gulped down another mug of hot chocolate. "Mrs. Claus likes to cook."

"You certainly have picked an odd place for those businesses," said Ivan and then he laughed heartily. "But I guess you have your reasons for coming this far north. I know I did when I came up here. I had some troubles with the royal families." Ivan volunteered.

"We have somewhat the same problem," Santa replied.

"You have come to the right part of the world then," Ivan said chuckling, leaning forward across the table and giving Santa a friendly slap on the shoulder.

"How can I help you?" continued Ivan, taking another big gulp of his hot cider.

"Well," Santa said slowly, "we are looking for a place that has some buildings that might be used for workshops. Obviously, we would like a house that is well-built and can keep the cold winds out."

"Will you need housing for all your men?" Ivan asked.

"No, once we find a place and get unloaded, they will return to the North Forest."

"I think I might know the perfect place for you. It's been empty for a number of years. However, it has a substantial house and a few large buildings. It was once owned by a company that made wagons and sleighs." Ivan continued, "Unfortunately, they had to transport their finished products too far to find any buyers. They eventually had to close."

"That sounds perfect," exclaimed Santa and Mrs. Claus nodded her head in approval.

"The nice thing about this place is its location", explained Ivan. "It is in the big valley. We call it Hidden Valley. There always seems to be a cloud of fog or an unusual mist that hangs over the valley. It makes it pretty difficult for many people to find the place. However, the effects of the fog and the valley make it pretty well protected against the harsh cold winds. It's not a pleasant journey to get there but when you are finally there, it is definitely comfortable down in the Valley." Ivan continued his description. "This sounds great!" exclaimed Santa as he grabbed Mrs. Claus's hand. "What do you think Mama?"

"It sounds very nice," Mrs. Claus answered.

"We would like to go see it. Could you give us directions?" inquired Santa with a twinge of excitement in his voice.

"I think it would be best if I take you there. It is a very difficult area to find if you do not know the exact landmarks." Ivan answered. "Be prepared. It's a nice place once you arrive, but it

is often an unpleasant ride to get there. If you want to be away from the populations, this is as far North as you can get. I would not be surprised if the actual location of the North Pole isn't somewhere in Hidden Valley."

"The North Pole?" inquired Santa. "What is that?"

"The North pole, why that is the most northern point in the world. Everything from there is south."

This intrigued Santa to be at the top of the world. He put his arm around Mrs. Claus and said quietly to her, "I think we might have found our new home."

"I hope so," she replied, "I am ready to get settled." They had been traveling for weeks and she was anxious to get back into a place of her own.

"I will also need some workers," Santa said as he turned back to Ivan. "Is there any place I can find some people that need work?"

"Ah, that might be a problem. As you can see, my poor wife Ingrid has to do most of the cooking with help from my daughter Eva. There are few people around that we can find to work for us. Most of the families in this area are lumberjacks or fishermen. They keep fairly well busy."

"Is there no one whom we might get to work for us?" inquired Santa. "There may be some, but remember, you are in the most secluded area of the world. Your only neighbors in Hidden Valley are the elfins. Unfortunately, they are not very reliable workers."

"Well, I would need many workers. If you don't mind, spread the word for me." said Santa. Ivan assured him that he would.

"Tell us more about the elfins," Mrs. Claus inquired.

"Oh, they just do not seem to be motivated to work," Ivan said hesitantly. "Oh fiddlesticks," piped in Ingrid who had been sitting next to Ivan. She turned and spoke directly to Mrs. Claus. "Ivan won't say a bad thing about anybody. The elfins are a miserable lot. They are short little people who do nothing but cause trouble. They live all throughout Hidden Valley."

"Oh no!" Mrs. Claus said putting her hand up to her mouth. This was a little bit discouraging information to hear about your new and only potential neighbors.

"Oh yes," continued Ingrid. "We could never get them to come out of the valley to work. Supposedly at one time they were a very friendly and industrious group of people. They're very small. They seem to have endless energy but unfortunately that energy is usually directed toward great mischief and tomfoolery."

"How do they exist?" inquired Santa.

Ingrid continued, "We do not really know. They live in small hovels for homes. We think they subsist mostly on berries and nuts."

"I've only been in the valley a few times over the years," interjected Ivan. "Their fields did not look healthy, and they seem to farm in a hap-hazard manner."

"They will steal things from you," Ingrid continued, "but not for the sake of taking something for themselves. Whatever they have stolen will usually show back up on your doorstep a few days later but they just love to make trouble. I do not see how you could depend on any of them to provide reliable work for you."

This was discouraging for both Santa and Mrs. Claus to hear. "Do you know what changed them from a friendly and industrious people to curmudgeons?"

"No," Ivan replied, "no one seems to know why they changed so much."

It was now late in the evening. Adam and the rest of the men and boys excused themselves and headed up to their rooms. They were exhausted, as usual, after a full day's ride on the wagons.

Santa and Mrs. Claus continued their conversation with Ivan, Ingrid, and Eva for another half hour before they retired for the evening. As they were climbing into bed, Santa and Mrs. Claus discussed the good and bad of what they had heard about the homestead in Hidden Valley. Santa finally blew out the candle on his bed stand, kissed Mrs. Claus goodnight and soon they were both snoring pleasantly.

Arriving in Hidden Valley

At the first signs of daylight, one could hear the wooden plank floors creaking as guests of the inn began to stir. Santa and Mrs. Claus sprang out of bed, dressed and went down to the dining area. After a good hearty breakfast, the men went out and hitched the teams of horses onto the wagons and brought them around to the front of the inn.

After a round of hugs with Ingrid and Eva, their new found friends, Santa and Mrs. Claus climbed up onto their wagons. Ivan climbed up on the lead wagon with Adam and waved to his wife and daughter as the caravan of wagons slowly rumbled away from the inn. The chill in the air was much more noticeable now. There were wisps of snowflakes in the air. Ivan was wearing a heavy winter coat with big furry gloves. He had advised everybody to dress warmly before they left the inn. The journey to Hidden Valley was to be approximately a half day's ride north of the inn. Ivan's description of the traveling conditions was correct. The roads were bumpy and hardly distinguishable in the low grasses. There were forest areas scattered here and there but the trees were much smaller and scrawnier than the massive trees the Clauses were accustomed to in the North Forest. Occasionally, they would see small herds of elk or reindeer grazing far off. Several times, Ivan stood up in the lead wagon to point to some distant area showing everybody a Bull Moose. Sometimes there would be the twitter of some very small birds flying overhead. The whole area was wide open and relatively desolate and the winds swept across the vast open areas.

The sky was dark and gray. After an hour of traveling, the winds started to increase in strength, enough to make the cold air sting the exposed cheeks of all the drivers. To protect herself from the cold North wind, Mrs. Claus wrapped around her shoulders the warm quilts given to her by the women back at their farm. Occasionally there were good strong gusts of wind, strong enough to slightly shake the big heavy wagons. With each gust, the horses would snort and bow their necks into the wind. Finally around midday, the caravan of wagons slowly moved through a wooded area just as a fog began to settle in over the group.

Ivan, sitting next to Adam in the lead wagon, had to lean forward while trying to get a better view of the road in front of them. The fog surrounded the small caravan of wagons, making it difficult to see anything more than just a few yards in front of the horses. The Clauses could see Ivan directing Adam with motions from his big gloved hands. Soon, they could feel the wagons making their way down a slow gradual incline. Then the cold blistering winds seemed to disappear. The wagons wound their way down a solid but winding road through thick evergreen trees. The roadway narrowed to the point where the evergreen branches swished along the sides of the wagons. With the fog making it difficult to see past the front of the horses and the trees very close to each side of the wagons, there became a feeling of security.

Shortly, the wagons came out of the fog to have a clear panoramic view of a quiet and pleasant valley. The Clauses were awestruck by the beauty of the valley. The trees appeared to be mostly blue spruces, with soft, pine-like branches. There were meadows interspersed among the patches of forest. The road widened and the ride became very smooth.

A few miles ahead, some roofs could be seen amidst the treetops. Ivan turned around towards the Clauses' wagon and pointed to the rooftops. One building, with a round roof, had what appeared to be a steeple at its center. In only a few minutes, the wagons passed through a group of evergreen trees and into a courtyard area in front of a large well-built log home. Santa saw immediately numerous chimneys indicating at least four, if not more, fireplaces inside. This house, just like the one in the North Forest, had an expansive front porch. It was as big, if not bigger than their previous home. As the wagons approached the house, Mrs. Claus excitedly grabbed Santa's arm.

Although the house was abandoned, she could envision the hominess this house could eventually provide. Santa was impressed also. He quickly scanned the other buildings. There were three large barn type buildings. Each constructed with a combination of stone foundations and log walls. The largest of the buildings was a huge octagon-shaped structure. The center of the roof had a large white steeple. He immediately knew this was exactly the place he had dreamed of owning.

There were a number of smaller houses surrounding the far side of the buildings. They appeared to be workers homes, small and fairly shabby looking. Most of these small houses looked like they had not been occupied or cared for in many years. The one thing that stood out about the main house and the smaller houses was the tasteful amount of gingerbread decoration on each one. The drabness of the smaller houses was purely the lack of paint. Santa and Mrs. Claus both thought to themselves that some tasteful coats of colorful paint would spruce up the little houses very nicely.

Ivan had been correct. Although the air was cool, it definitely did not have the stinging cold

bite they had experienced from the winds just before they moved down into the valley. The wagons pulled up to the front of the big house. Santa helped Mrs. Claus down from the wagons while the men and boys jumped down from each of theirs. They all tromped up a short set of steps to the front porch. There were leaves and small branches scattered across the heavy smooth planks of the porch floor. The shutters were closed on the windows.

Ivan reached up and pulled a key out from one of the niches in the log siding. He unlocked the door and stood back to allow Santa and Mrs. Claus to enter the house and the others followed. They were immediately met with the friendly aroma of cedar. A heavy wooden staircase led upstairs. Santa and Mrs. Claus walked straight ahead into a magnificent living room and dining room area. The walls were thick curly pine. The solid oak floors had a shiny worn look to them. Two huge oversized fireplaces that dominated the walls stretched to each end of the room.

Mrs. Claus's eyes were wide with delight. "How do you like it, Mama?"asked Santa.

"Oh, this is wonderful!" she replied happily as she pushed through two swinging doors going into the kitchen area. "Santa, come quickly," he heard her call. "Look at the ovens!" she exclaimed. "They are bigger than the ones we have at home." She was bustling around the kitchen opening cupboard doors and drawers. Santa saw the look of delight on her face, something he had not seen for many months. He knew they had found their new home!

"How many rooms are upstairs?" Santa called to the boys who had impatiently scampered up the stairs.

"We count ten rooms," one of them responded from somewhere upstairs. "Oh good," thought Santa knowing he would want to have good accommodations if anyone traveled all that way to visit them. The interior of the house sprang to life as the men moved around the outside of the house opening up the shutters. Light flowed in showing details of everything on the first floor.

"I am sure this was an inn when the previous owners occupied the property," said Ivan. The excessively large kitchen area and living/dining area seemed to confirm that. "I hope you like what you see!" Ivan said over his shoulder, as he placed wood in the fireplace and began to start a fire. In a few moments he had a nice roaring fire going in both fireplaces, warming up the room.

Mrs. Claus went from room to room envisioning where to put everything. The more she saw, the more pleased she became. She wanted to continue her investigation of the magnificent house but she knew the men were hungry.

She had Peter, the oldest of the boys, start the fire in the fireplace in the kitchen. She sent the other boys out to the wagons to start bringing in food supplies. She knew she would have to get busy preparing a lunch. She started cleaning the kitchen.

Outside, the men unhitched the teams and walked them to the stable barn. Santa went with them. "Well, how about that!" exclaimed Eric. "We have lost three or four lanterns on the trip and maybe one or two bell straps. They must have brushed off as we came through that narrow stretch on the way down," he surmised. The others looked at the wagons, confirming a few of the lanterns were missing.

"Elfins," Ivan blurted out, everyone turned to him. "The elfins are probably up to their mischief" he pointed past the surrounding buildings to further on down the valley. There were little columns of smoke from the chimneys of the houses that could be seen scattered here and there.

"Will Santa have to worry about the thievery around here?" Adam asked.

"Not really," replied Ivan. "Whatever they have taken will probably show up someplace soon. They never really keep anything. They just want to show they can take things if they wanted to, maybe just to get your attention." Everybody kind of chuckled and began taking the harnesses off the horses and leading them into the barn.

Santa was anxious to see what the buildings looked like inside and the others joined him. He and Adam followed Ivan across the small square and up the sloping ramp of the large octagonal building. It dominated the little cluster of buildings. Ivan pushed open one of the large sliding barn doors and then pushed open the other side. The daylight illuminated the inside. Santa clapped his hands together as he viewed the many workbenches around the sides of the building. There were two balconies each exhibiting more workbenches for what had apparently been an active wagon and sleigh manufacturing operation at one time. The main floor had two large fireplaces, with what appeared to be equipment for a blacksmith. Santa was exhilarated. Ivan could see his excitement. "I told you this would be what you were looking for!" he exclaimed, proud of himself for being correct.

"This is excellent!" exclaimed Santa, "excellent!" Santa was as giddy as a schoolboy. He bounded up the stairs to see what each balcony looked like. All the others looked around with amazement. "You'll have plenty of room to store toys in here, Santa," one of them shouted up to Santa, who was making a trip all the way around the second floor balcony. After completely exploring the building, everybody followed Santa to the other two large buildings surrounding the small courtyard square. They also had many workbenches and places to put tools. Santa could not have been more pleased.

They finished their exploring by wandering through the cluster of small houses that were nestled among the trees. Although not very big, each was well built and had a nice fireplace. They looked as though it had been years since any work had been done on them, leaving them in a state of dispair.

"What nice little places! They could be fixed up for workers and their families if I could only

find good workers," Santa said to no one in particular. The men nodded in agreement but nobody answered with any solutions. The banging of some pans and the voice of Mrs. Claus yelling, "Come and eat!" started the small group back across the square towards the main house. When they arrived, there were sandwiches and hot chocolate ready for them in the big dining area. As a group, they sat down in front of the fires and ate heartily.

"Well, I'd better think about heading back before the sun starts to set," said Ivan.

After chewing a big bite of sandwich, Santa wiped his mouth with his napkin, as he knew not to talk with a mouth full of food, and said, "We will unload one of the smaller wagons right after lunch. You can take that back to the inn. However, would you not rather stay the night and get a fresh start in the morning?" Santa asked. "We can have the bedrooms upstairs pretty well furnished before evening."

"Thank you Santa, but I'd better get back and make sure the girls are keeping everyone at the inn well fed." replied Ivan with a chuckle in his voice. They finished their lunch. The men and the boys went out to the wagons and began to carry things into the house. Mrs. Claus directed them as to where to place everything. Ivan and Santa sat in the dining room finishing the details of Santa's purchase of the property. Mrs. Claus clasped her hands together with a very delighted look upon her face. She rushed over and gave Santa a kiss on the cheek and scurried back into the kitchen.

"Do you want one of the boys to ride back with you?" Santa asked Ivan as they had concluded their business.

"No, that will not be necessary. I've made the trip before. Besides, it gives me the opportunity to sing my favorite songs at the top of my lungs without offending anybody's ears." Ivan said laughingly, flashing a grin from behind his red mustache and beard. Santa knew he had made a good friend in Ivan. Ivan felt the same way about Santa and Mrs. Claus.

Soon, one of the smaller wagons was emptied and the horses hitched. The group gathered around to shake Ivan's hand and bid him farewell. He got up on the wagon, flicked the reins and waved to everybody as the wagon began moving slowly across the small courtyard onto the road back to the Elfinland Inn.

The remaining wagons were finally unloaded, and the furniture placed throughout the house. Mrs. Claus's cooking utensils and supplies were stored in the kitchen. Santa's toy making tools and plenty of supplies were stored in the big octagonal barn. Everything was finished by the time the early darkness arrived. The temperature dropped through the day, making the roaring fireplaces in the house that much more inviting. After a nice hearty meal of Mrs. Claus's special stew, they sat around the dinner table in front of the fire, just as they would have done had they been at the North Forest farm, and discussed all the events of the past few days. Soon the men drifted upstairs to get a goodnight's sleep. Santa and Mrs. Claus headed for bed themselves.

Santa blew out the candle on his nightstand, then slid under the covers.

"Do you like the place?" He asked Mrs. Claus in the darkness.

"Oh yes Santa," she answered him. "I just love this place. I could not be happier."

"You know it might be lonely up here. There aren't that many people around."

"We will make do," she answered. "We always have." In a matter of minutes they were both snoring softly.

Santa woke up with the first rays of daylight coming through the window. He could hear Mrs. Claus already clanking pots and pans in the kitchen. Hearing voices, he knew some of the men must already be up and about. He went downstairs and for a hearty breakfast with his men. Mrs. Claus was bustling in and out of the kitchen making sure everyone had enough food on their plate and their mugs were full of hot chocolate.

After breakfast, the men went into the stables to do some simple maintenance of the wagons. The men hitched up all the wagons except one large wagon they would be leaving with Santa.
Too soon came the time that both Santa and Mrs. Claus were dreading. The men and boys would be leaving them. The next time they would see each other was an unknown. Mrs. Claus kept suggesting they stay for another few days, but she realized they had been away from their families for many weeks and wanted to get back. As the wagons were being prepared, Mrs. Claus got busy making sandwiches and hot pots of chocolate for them to put under the wagons seats.

The time had finally come. With tears streaming down Mrs. Claus's face, she hugged and kissed each one goodbye. Santa shook hands with each one and then gave them each a big bear hug as well. He said goodbye to every one of them as a father would say goodbye to his sons. Soon they all climbed up on the wagons and quietly waved to their good friends and disappeared through the evergreen trees, leaving Santa and Mrs. Claus waving to them from the front porch. For a long time all was quiet on the wagons as the men and boys wrestled with their sadness and the lumps on their hearts.

Santa and Mrs. Claus stood quietly on the front porch after the wagons were out of sight. Mrs. Claus's eyes were misty and a small tear slowly rolled down her cheek. Santa gazed across the little courtyard square. The octagonal building and other buildings sat empty and quiet across the little courtyard. The small houses could be seen amongst the snow-clad evergreens. Several squirrels were playing in the trees. But no other creature could be seen in any direction. What will be our future here, thought Santa. Soon, Mrs. Claus reached for Santa's hand and they both walked back into the house. The Clauses were at their new home, the North Pole.

DISCOVERING THE ELVES

When you think of the North Pole, who do you usually think about? Santa and his elves! But have you ever thought of where the elves came from? Most people do not. The elves just seem to have always been there. But that was not the case. Remember that Santa and Mrs. Claus had been warned about the unfriendly and mischievous nature of the elfins.

Santa and Mrs. Claus spent a relatively quiet time by themselves, in the cluster of deserted buildings that was now their new home. Three days passed before they saw any other people. Two hunters knocked on their front door, asking if there were still rooms available in the inn. Santa had to inform them this was now a private home but welcomed them in for one of Mrs. Claus's delicious meals and let them stay in the upstairs bedrooms for the night. They were told they were welcome to stay anytime. Both Santa and Mrs. Claus were happy just to be able to talk with somebody new.

Their friendship with these hunters, Hanson and Cleave proved to be beneficial through the years. They would often drop off a deer after some of their hunting expeditions, providing Mrs. Claus with venison for her delicious stew. Other than that, the first week of living in their new home was very quiet. The only other meaningful event was Santa walking out the front door one morning and finding four lanterns and two straps of bells on the front porch. What Ivan had said about the elfins was true.

Whatever items they took, they eventually brought back. What a strange group these elfins must be, Santa pondered.

Several days later, Mrs. Claus was enjoying her large kitchen. The ovens were big, providing enough space to cook any number of delicious foods. She had cooked several apple pies, Santa's favorite, and placed the pies on the back porch railing to cool. A little while later when she went to retrieve them, she saw that one pie had two pieces cut out. The odd thing was that they were not two pieces cut side-by-side. They were cut opposite each other. "Oh that Santa," she thought. She swiftly walked to the front of the house and opened the front door. Stepping out onto the front porch, she yelled across the courtyard, knowing Santa was working in the big octagon barn. "You could not wait until lunch for your pie?" She yelled in a friendly voice. She heard the clanking of his tools stop for a moment. He yelled something back but it was muffled, she didn't understand what he said. It didn't matter. She had made the pies for him anyway. He was often known to sneak a piece pie or a piece of cake well before meal time. Grinning, she went back in and continued working in the kitchen. A little while later, she went back out on the back porch to bring in the cooled pies.

This time, however she heard some slight noises coming from the big wooden firewood box on the porch. Squirrels, she thought. She opened the lid and immediately let out a loud shriek. Santa, who was just coming in the front door, heard her and quickly rushed onto the back porch. "What is it?" he asked.

"I don't know," she replied in a slightly shaky voice. She pointed to the closed wooden box. "There is something strange looking in there."

Santa grabbed a rolling pin off the kitchen counter just in case there was a dangerous animal inside the box. He carried it with him over to the wooden box and quickly raised the lid. He was startled to find not one but two little creatures with pitiful scrunched-up faces. They had big noses, wrinkled looking skin and wide scared eyes, not to mention their pointed ears. Santa let out a quick "Yikes!" The two little critters squealed up to him, "Yikes!" as they were just as afraid of him as he was of them!

He stepped away as the two little creatures climbed out of the wooden box. They looked like two wee-little tiny wrinkled-up old men. Santa dropped the rolling pin once he realized there was no real danger to Mrs. Claus, and grabbed both of the creatures by the back of their pants. While Santa was holding them up in the air, their little legs kept churning as if they were running a race! "What are you doing here?" Santa demanded.

"Let us go, round fat man!" one of them said in great haste.

Santa looked at Mrs. Claus and said "They must be the elfins that Ivan had told us about. Fat man? They certainly have no manners whatsoever!"

"What is the meaning of you stealing our food?" Mrs. Claus asked with as bold a voice as she could muster.

"We were going to pay for it," the bigger of the two replied. "Look in the box, our pouch, we would have paid." Both of the creature's legs were still running and arms were flailing as Santa was holding them up in the air. Mrs. Claus looked into the wooden box and found a pouch. She pulled it up and opened it. It was full of nuts.

"What should we do with them?" Santa asked Mrs. Claus. "Do you think we should eat them?"

He asked as he winked at her.

"Oh no!" squealed the smaller of the two. "Please, we were hungry and we had not smelled anything as good as those pies in years!" Both of them had arms flailing as Santa still held onto them. Santa walked over to the dining table, still holding onto them. The little one, almost in tears, said to the other, Clarence, I knew we would get in trouble, I just knew we were gonna get into trouble."

Santa sat them down in chairs at the big dining room table noticing that their eyes just barely reached the top of the table. Santa continued to talk in a gruff manner, but Mrs. Claus could see the fear in the eyes of these pitiful sad faces. Before Santa could say anything more, Mrs. Claus asked, "Are you hungry?" Both of them looked up at her and nodded vigorously. "Okay, both of you sit right here. Santa, why don't you throw another log on the fire?" Santa obeyed, while wondering what type of existence this was going to be with such unusual little people as their only neighbors.

Mrs. Claus came back out of the kitchen with two plates filled with large pieces of apple pie. She also brought in two large mugs of hot chocolate topped off with marshmallows. As soon as she set the plates and silverware on the table, the two little elfins gobbled their pieces of pie in record time. Obviously, they were very hungry. "Would you like some more?" she asked. Again, they both nodded their heads vigorously. Mrs. Claus went back to the kitchen and brought out two more large pieces for them.

Their clothing was tattered, and they were obviously very hungry. Who knows the last time they had such scrumptious pie as only Mrs. Claus could make. The smaller of the two had a hole in his shoe with his big toe sticking out. Overall, these were very unattractive and a bit scary looking at first but once Santa and Mrs. Claus looked a little deeper, they saw they were just like us, and were hungry for some really good food.

"Why did you not just ask us for some food?" Santa inquired.

"We were afraid," replied the bigger one. "The last group of people here were very mean and nasty." That made Santa chuckle to himself. That seemed like the pot calling the kettle black from what he had been told.

"What are your names?" Mrs. Claus asked.

"My name is Clarence," said the bigger one. "This here is Freddy." "Nice to meet you Clarence and Freddie, this is Santa and I am Mrs.Claus. I imagine you know the difference between right and wrong. Stealing is wrong. You should know better. How old are you?" It was hard to tell how old these boys or men were.

I think I am 140 or maybe 141. Freddy is around 63 years old," Mrs. Claus gasped lightly. "As elfins, age does not affect us very much."

His answer did not faze Santa. Neither he nor Mrs. Claus seemed to age much through the years.

As they were talking, both Clarence and Freddie scarfed down large pieces of pie very quickly. They ate a third piece and drank four large mugs of hot chocolate with marshmallows.

Both Santa and Mrs. Claus noticed that as Clarence and Freddie ate, the appearance of both of them seem to improve noticeably. Their faces were smoother and the unfriendly demeanor disappeared from their eyes. Their lips became a little fuller, making the sneering effect less noticeable. Their skin gained a more healthy color. It could've been because they were cold and hungry, but the change seemed a little bit more than just that. Their unfriendly mannerisms and voice tones seem to disappear.

"You were going to pay for the pieces of pie with some nuts?" Santa asked.

"That is all that we had," answered Freddie. "We are very sorry." "What type of work do you do?" Santa inquired. This question seemed to perk up both Clarence and Freddie.

"We can do most anything, carpentry work, any sort of repair work, tending horses and reindeer, painting, stonework, anything you want done, we can do." Santa was still skeptical. Everything else Ivan had described about elfins had come to pass. Santa, a person who usually gives everyone the benefit of the doubt, would have to be shown by the elfins they had good work habits.

After three large pieces of pie, both Clarence and Freddie were feeling a little bit lethargic. Without saying anything, both of them slid down from their chairs. They walked over to the wooden benches against the walls and lay down flat on their backs. Within seconds, they were both snoring loudly. Santa and Mrs. Claus looked at each other and chuckled. "Odd little fellows," stated Santa.

Mrs. Claus laughed. "That was terrible of you to say we were going to eat them." She scoffed at Santa. "Did you see the look of fear in their eyes?" Santa laughed. "I was trying to put some fear into them. I did not want the scoundrels stealing my food every day." He looked over to where they were sleeping. "Do we just leave them there?" "Certainly," replied Mrs. Claus. "You go about your business. They will be all right here. I think they were just hungry. Did you notice how they looked so much better after they gobbled down your pie?" "Yes," Santa mused, "I did notice not only did they improve quite a bit in appearance, but they had a much friendlier attitude after they ate. I think you're right, they must've just been hungry." Santa went out the front door. He strolled back over to his new workshop. Mrs. Claus pulled some small quilts out of the closet and put them over the elfins. She smiled as she listened to the atrocious sound of their snoring.

It was a several hours later when Santa decided to take a break. After walking in the front door, he noticed the folded quilts on the benches where the little elfins had been sleeping. They were nowhere to be seen. He heard Mrs. Claus in the kitchen. When he entered, he gave her a quick little hug and saw she was making a half a dozen more pies. "Aw, good!" Santa exclaimed. "I didn't get any pie the last time I was here. Where is the other pie? I sure am hungry." He looked around the kitchen and glanced out at the back porch railing but did not see it.

"I sold it," Mrs. Claus said cheerfully.

"You sold it?" Santa asked with a playful tone in his voice.

"Yes, Clarence and Freddie paid me for it. They said they had family back home that would love to have some of my pie. They said they had never tasted anything so delicious."

"Oooh, I'm going to be so hungry," Santa said with false sincerity. "How much did they pay you?"

Mrs. Claus pointed to the little bag of nuts sitting on the counter. Santa chuckled. "And I am selling them some more tomorrow," she said waving her hand over the pies she was currently making. "I drove a hard bargain. These are costing them two big baskets of nuts." Mrs. Claus was thinking ahead about making some of Santa's favorite nut bread. "These nuts have a good taste to them." She cut Santa a big slab of bread from a loaf she had already baked, spread some blackberry jam on it and handed it to him. He wouldn't starve to death while he was standing in her kitchen.

"Also," she continued, "they wanted to know if there was any work they could do around here. I told them to come back tomorrow with the nuts and talk with you." Santa had his doubts about their work abilities but he did need somebody to clean out the stables and he would also like to start cleaning up the work areas in the buildings. "Okay, we will see how well they work, but I'm not committing to anything permanent yet."

"I know," Mrs. Claus replied as she patted him on the shoulder. "Let's see how they work. They said they would be here bright and early tomorrow."

Santa was up early the next day. However, he had already had his breakfast and was working in his workshop before the elfins finally arrived. "Bright and early?" he thought to himself. Half the morning was already gone. When they did finally arrive, he did notice there were eight of them this time, dragging four big baskets full of nuts. It looked like they had brought their wives and the smaller little people apparently were their children. Led by Clarence, they dragged the four baskets around to the back of the house to the back porch.

Santa completed the last details of the toys he was just finishing and wiped off his hands. He then headed across the courtyard to the house. By the time he walked in, Mrs. Claus was already feeding them a nice breakfast at the big table next to the fire. Santa noticed that Clarence and Freddie looked much better this morning. They had a bit more color in their faces and their arms and hands appeared more muscular. However, the lady elfins were grey in color and had a gaunt complexion that Santa and Mrs. Claus had first noticed about Clarence and Freddie. The children looked up at Santa as he walked in with wide-eyed wonder. "Ho Ho Ho!" Santa welcomed them. It seems that you have brought me a bigger work crew. Both Clarence and Freddie immediately got up out of their

seats and went to Santa to shake his hand. Santa noticed that Mrs. Claus had put folded quilts on the seats of all the chairs so all could reach the table easily.

"Yes sir," Clarence volunteered, "we would like to repay you for your kindness and understanding yesterday. What work can we do for you today?" Before Santa could reply, Mrs. Claus came out of the kitchen with a tray full of hot cinnamon buns and hot chocolate to go with the eggs and bacon she had already served on their plates.

"Hello dear," she said cheerfully, "your work crew is here." She set the tray down in front of everybody and filled the hot chocolate mugs. The elfins eyed the cinnamon buns but did not move. She saw them hesitate. "Please, take them. They will give you energy." They all immediately grabbed a bun in each hand and made excited giggling noises.

Clarence turned back to Santa and said, "Let me introduce you to my wife Pixie and Freddie's wife, Suzy. My children, Peter and Skeeter, and these are Freddie's children Toby and Tammy." Santa circled around the table shaking each one's wee little hand.

"I wanted to feed them first," said Mrs. Claus. "They dragged four nice baskets full of nuts all the way here this morning. Clarence said it took them about an hour to get here and they hadn't had very much to eat before they left home."

"Quite all right," said Santa, seeing the appreciative look in their wives' eyes. "Get yourself well fed. I am sure I can find plenty of things that need to be done around here today."

"Oh thank you," said Freddie. "We are more than anxious to repay you for your and Mrs. Claus's kindness."

Their meal finished, Santa gave them instructions to clean the stables, where the four workhorses remained. He had put them out in the pasture behind the house earlier that morning.. Santa thought that cleaning the stables would be a big enough job for all of them to do for the rest of the day. "What else needs to be done?" questioned Clarence.

"That should be enough for today," Santa replied, anticipating an unhurried day of work.

"Well," inquired Clarence again, "if we get done with the stables, what else would you like to have done today?" Santa pulled on his beard thoughtfully and then pointed across the courtyard to one of the smaller work buildings. "That building needs to have all the workbenches and floors cleaned." There were a lot of scrap boards and metal pieces scattered throughout the buildings, apparently leftover scraps from the wagon building business. "Okay, and that building over there also?" Clarence pointed toward the other work building.

"Yes, eventually we can get to that one, but it is not very urgent to get to." Santa figured it would be a few days before they could get to the other building. Each building was going to be a big undertaking to get cleaned up.

finally got it perfect when he felt he was being watched. He looked up to find the elfins watching him with wide-eyed amazement. Especially the little elfins, their eyes as huge as pies. They stood transfixed while watching Santa pull the little duck toy across the broad smooth plank floor of his work area.

He immediately remembered the joy his toys had brought to the children back on his North Forest farm. Although, he did not have many toys, he asked the little elfins if they would each like a toy. They each bounced around with uncontrolled excitement. "Oh sir, no!" begged Pixie. "We could never repay you for your kindness."

"Do not worry," replied Santa. He was gazing around the workshop, which was now immaculately clean. The wood railings on the balconies were wiped clean and had a glossy shine. The floors were spotless. There was not a speck of dirt or dust in the whole building. "You have done far more than expected. I am very pleased." He then turned to the children and pointed to the pile of toys. "Each of you grab a toy."

The little elfin children were bouncing with joyful energy. Peter found a big wagon. Skeeter pulled a rocking horse from the pile. Little Tammy found a baby doll and Toby quickly hugged the quacking duck Santa had just been working on. They danced around, falling over and laid on the ground jiggling, giggling and laughing. It was a good reminder for Santa for why he was making all the toys. Each of them ran over and hugged Santa. Of course, they were so little, they were actually hugging his knee. But each would spread out their arms with their little palms facing up, wiggling their fingers, indicating Santa to bend down so they could each give him a kiss on the cheek.

Pixie and Suzy watched with tears in their eyes. Even Clarence and Freddie were misty eyed. "Another thing," Santa said, as he put his hands on Clarence and Freddie's shoulder. "No more 'sir', my name is Santa." From that time on the elfins and the Clauses became fast friends.

That night, as they were blowing out the candles and getting into bed Santa confessed to Mrs. Claus, "I made a mistake about these people. They seem very competent and trustworthy. I should not have listened to what other people thought about them until I met them myself."

"Don't be too hard on yourself Santa," Mrs. Claus replied. "Remember, before they had some good meals in themselves, they did have a very un- friendly demeanor." She continued, "I hope you are planning to keep them on full-time. I could use Pixie and Suzy in the house helping with the chores."

"Yes," replied Santa, "they seem to be very reliable and amazingly fast. I hope that continues."

After several minutes of lying under the covers, reminiscing about the day, both are quietly snoring away.

More Elfins

Santa knew that he would need more workers, but he did not expect the method of recruiting that happened. Each evening, he checked to make sure the horse stalls were latched and that the horses had been fed properly during the day. However, the next few mornings he would find the stall doors unlatched and partially open. The horses were wandering freely around the barn. At first, he thought maybe Clarence and Freddie were being forgetful, but when he checked each night, the gates were closed properly. This puzzled Santa.

On the third morning, he heard a little rustle of hay in the loft overhead. He now understood what was happening. "Who's up there," he yelled. There was some scurrying around up above and panicky little squeaky noises. All of a sudden, two little bodies plunked down from the upper rafters through the hole next to the ladder. They landed with a thud and created a cloud of dust on the straw-filled floor near Santa's feet. They immediately jumped up and scrambled around, running into each other and falling back down. Back on their feet, they tried running out the door, but got tangled up in a strand of rope that was lying on the floor. Santa quickly strolled over and picked them both up from the back of their pants. He carried them out of the stables, arms and legs flailing around, to Mrs. Claus's back porch. "Mama," he yelled, "I've got two more. Can I put them down the well?" Both bodies let out a little whimpering scream when they heard him say that. They continued to flail their arms and legs trying to get free from Santa's grasp.

"Oh Santa," Mrs. Claus scolded as she came out onto the back porch, wiping her hands on her apron. "You are scaring the daylights out of them. Bring them in so we can give them something to eat." At the same table where only a few days before the Clauses had met Clarence and Freddie, they now met Hector and Bobbit. Both were in the same condition that Clarence and Freddie had been. Their skin was ashen, wrinkled and unhealthy looking. They too had big noses, pointy ears, and a frightened look in their eyes. Mrs. Claus fed them a healthy breakfast of eggs, bacon, and pancakes with plenty of syrup. She poured five or six large mugs of hot chocolate before they were eventually satisfied.

Santa remembered the routine. "So, you were trying to steal our horses?"

Both of the elfins looked at Santa in shock. "Oh, no sir," Hector cried, "we were trying to steal one of your pies!" Bobbit took his hat off and smacked Hector on the head. "Be quiet you goofball!"

Both Santa and Mrs. Claus chuckled at these two. Mrs. Claus went back out to the kitchen and brought in a large piece of pie for each of them. They immediately gobbled it down so fast, Mrs. Claus had to get each of them another large piece of pie. Just as before, when they had finished their meal, their physical appearance and behavior had improved greatly.

"Please," they begged, "is there something we can do to repay you?"

"Yes there is," replied Santa. "Do you know how to repair fences?" Both of them nodded their heads energetically.

He had them follow him out to the back porch. Santa pointed to the fence that surrounded the large pasture behind the house. The fence followed the shape of the land for quite a few acres. He gave them instructions on how he would like to have the posts straightened and the cross timbers securely fastened to each post. Although the fence was in reasonably good shape, there were many sections where the boards and posts needed repair.

Providing Hector and Bobbit with shovels, hammer and nails, and pry bars, he sent them out into the back pasture.

When Clarence and Freddie arrived with their families Santa questioned Clarence about the character of Hector and Bobbitt. "They are good workers when they aren't experiencing hard times." answered Clarence. That was good enough for Santa. Clarence and Freddie proceeded with doing their chores, feeding the horses and hauling off debris they had collected when cleaning the work buildings the previous day. The ladies and the children went inside the house to help Mrs. Claus. Santa settled in at his workbench and proceeded to work on more toys.

It was on this day that Santa and Mrs. Claus made an important discovery about elfins. At lunchtime, Mrs. Claus stepped out on the back porch and rang the bell bringing everyone to the house for lunch. Hector and Bobbitt scurried out from the far corner of the field. They were climbing up the back steps as Santa came out onto the back porch. "How far have you gotten?" he asked the elfins. Hector turned and pointed down the fence line to where they had left the shovels leaning against a fence post. It was much further than Santa had expected. He was pleasantly surprised how straight and even the fence was where they had worked. It appeared as if they were able to get about one fourth of the fence repaired during the hours they had worked that morning.

Santa motioned them through the back door, past the kitchen and into the dining room. Hector and Bob were pleased to see Clarence and Freddie and their families. They all sat down with

Santa and Mrs. Claus at the dining room table and had a hearty meal. When they were finished, Mrs. Claus noticed the children glancing around the room intensely. They were looking for something. "Would you like some candy?" she asked them. At that, all the elfins' ears wiggled uncontrollably. She laughed, going into the kitchen and returning with a big bowl of candy. They quickly grabbed candy as she passed around the bowl, then all returned to their chores.

Santa was enjoying his work at his workbench. He had designed some new toys and was inspecting his latest work. Occasionally, he would walk over to the big open doors to see if he could catch a glimpse of what everybody was doing. Clarence and Freddie scurried about,   taking care of small projects. Occasionally, Pixie and Suzy would bring some small rugs out to the front porch of a house and beat the dust out of them, then hang them over the railing. Santa was pleased with how things were working out.

In the latter part of the afternoon, but not too late, Hector and Bobbitt came wondering around the corner of the house, carrying the shovels and hammers. Santa's first reaction was that these two fellows were not very hard workers, apparently wanting to quit early in the day. He watched them approaching his work area through the open doors. He got up from his bench and met them at the doorway. "You didn't want to work very long today," he chided them.

"We finished the fence," said Bobbitt. This seemed impossible to Santa. "Let's go see," he said to them as they put down their shovels, leaning them up against the doorway. They strolled across the courtyard and around the back of the house and to Santa's amazement the fence was in perfect condition all the way around the pasture. He could not believe it. They did four times the work this afternoon as they had done that morning, and Santa felt they had done much more work than he expected that morning. He was amazed that they could have finished so quickly.

"It looks great!" he exclaimed. "How did you finish so quickly?" Both of them just shrugged their shoulders. "Come," he said putting his arm around each of their shoulders, "this deserves another piece of pie." They all climbed the back steps and rewarded themselves with a big piece of pie, including Santa.

"What else can we do?" Hecter asked.

Santa pondered for a minute stroking his white beard. "I do need to have my tools sharpened. Do either of you have experience doing that?" Both of them nodded eagerly. They spent the rest of the afternoon taking many of Santa's tools, sharpening the blades, oiling the moving parts, and polishing wooden handles. Santa noticed how they each handled the tools with great respect. Once again, he was very pleased with the results when they were finished.

As dinnertime approached, everyone headed back to the house. When Santa arrived, he noticed the many scraps of fabric on one of the dining room tables. Pixie and Suzy and the children had on new outfits. Their faces were beaming. When Clarence and Freddie came in through the front door, Pixie and Suzy rushed to meet them with a little stack of   clothing. They made their husbands go upstairs immediately and put them on. Hector and Bobbitt followed Santa into the dining room. Mrs. Claus met them with a little stack of clothing. Hector and Bobbitt's outfits showed much wear and tear also. Mrs. Claus instructed them to go upstairs and change. The dinner that night consisted of a lot of oohing and aahing as each displayed their new clothing outfits. Clarence and Freddie and their families looked remarkably better than when they had first arrived just a few days ago. Faces were rosier. The sneers were now friendly smiles. The sinister eyes had converted to wide-eyed happy eyes. In a remarkably short period of time, both families looked dramatically healthier, no "wrinkledy" skin.

That night, as Santa and Mrs. Claus were getting into bed, Santa made an observation. "I am truly amazed at the speed our newfound friends are capable of completing tasks. I have noticed that when they eat their fill of candy, they appear to be able to get things accomplished in much shorter time frames than could be expected."

"Ha," Mrs. Claus retorted, "funny to hear that coming from you Santa!" He was often questioned on how he got things done that seemed impossible for normal explanation. "But I agree. I could see their delight with candy has a definite effect on their energy levels for the rest of the day. I have one simple suggestion."

"What is that?" Santa inquired as he was blowing out the candles on his nightstand.

"We always make sure we have plenty of candy available," said Mrs. Claus. This made Santa chuckle. He knew one of Mrs. Claus's most favorite activities was making candy.

"We will work on that," soon both were snoring away.

The Elves to the Rescue

The loneliness that Mrs. Claus had first experienced when arriving at their new home in Hidden Valley was quickly disappearing. The elfins were becoming very close friends to her. She found they were as loyal and trustworthy a people as her friends back in the North Forest. Although they were small, they had the same feelings and concerns as anyone else. If you treated them well, they treated you very well. Pixie and Suzy were special to her and companions as they worked together in the kitchen. They were extremely good seamstresses. What they didn't know, they were very anxious to learn. Both Pixie and Suzy greatly appreciated the generosity of Mrs. Claus. Like any female, they wanted to be attractive. Although their appearance could be described as comical to big people, they looked normal to each other. Mrs. Claus's gifts of brushes and combs, soaps and creams, scarves and hats reinstated a sense of pride in their appearance. The conversations they had mirrored the conversations she would have had with her good friends back in the North Forest

Santa was feeling the same way about his men. Clarence appeared to be a community leader for the elfins. He became Santa's number one helper for running the operations around the small cluster of buildings. He could depend on Clarence and Freddie to take care of the things that needed to be done without Santa having to instruct every detail. The respect and trust continued to grow between the men. And it was fortunate to have Clarence around when disaster hit!

That came on a day when the only unusual event was the arrival of the supply wagon. Santa had made arrangements with his good friend, Ivan back at the Elfinland Inn, to have a regularly scheduled supply wagon make the trip up to Hidden Valley. The wagon rumbled in early in the morning. It was loaded with a new supply of sugar, cinnamon, chocolate, and many assortments of materials for making candy. After it was unloaded, Mrs. Claus and her elfin helpers spent the morning putting the supplies away. They immediately made plans for making a new batch of candy. The rest of the wagon was unloaded in Santa's workshop. He had requested a large supply of paint and materials for making toys. Once the wagon was unloaded and on its way back to the Elfinland Inn, life returned back to normal.

It was late in the morning when Mrs. Claus realized Santa had not made his usual periodic visit to the kitchen. Leaving Pixie and Suzy working on a batch of candy, she took a tray with a mug of hot chocolate and cinnamon buns to take out to Santa. As she stepped through the open doors into his workbench area, her heart immediately dropped. As we know, Santa is usually a robust and happy person. He had the knack to make everyone around him feel happy. His legendary "Ho Ho Ho!" would brighten up any occasion. But as Mrs. Claus approached his workbench, she saw Santa sitting at his bench leaning forward with his head in his hands. "What is wrong?" She asked quickly setting the tray down in front of him, then putting her arms around him from behind.

"Oh mama," he said in a very despondent voice, "I am doomed!" "What makes you say that?" She asked in her quiet and soothing voice.

Without looking up, Santa patted a big leather bound book sitting on his bench.

"Your list of children? What is wrong with that? You have the list every year." She inquired.

"I know," he replied, "but look at it. It is 10 times larger than it was last year." That was true. Each year his story of generosity for providing gifts to children on December 25th was becoming known to a greater number of families far and wide.

"I knew I might be stretching some of my magic powers moving up here this year and still having time to make the toys for children." Very rarely did Santa mention the word magic to anybody other than Mrs. Claus. "But I was estimating it would be approximately the same number of children as last year."

"Why don't you just make them for the same children as last year?" She asked.

"Oh no, I couldn't do that," Santa replied. "Think of all the children who would be anticipating something from Santa this year, only to find they did not get anything. Can you imagine their disappointment?"

Mrs. Claus saw the dilemma. She patted him on the back, "Don't worry, we will think of something."

"I don't know," Santa said with a sense of resignation. "I did not make plans for this type of situation. I don't know what to do." He sat there just shaking his head.

Mrs. Claus left Santa sitting at his bench. As she stepped back out into the courtyard, she saw Clarence coming out of one of the other buildings. She waved at him to meet her across the courtyard at the house. They met at the front steps at the same time. "Clarence, I need your help." She said as they were walking up the steps toward the front door. "Certainly Mrs. Claus, I will be glad to do anything for you."

"It's not for me. It is for Santa," she explained as they went through the front door and walked into the dining room. "Here, sit down." They both sat down across from each other at the dining room table. She told him the story of how Santa delivered toys to children all over the North country every year. But this year, the number of people on Santa's list had grown dramatically. Santa was now in a predicament. He could never make enough toys to get to all the children by December 25th this year. Clarence nodded in understanding. "Don't worry Mrs. Claus," he said. "I do not think the problem is as serious as you might think. I will go talk with Santa right now. And may I have some candy?" She smiled and brought a large handful of candy for him from the kitchen.

When Clarence walked into the building Santa was still sitting with his head in his hands at his workbench. "Santa, my good friend, I understand you think you have a little problem." Clarence exclaimed as he pulled up a chair across from him, putting several blocks of wood on the chair so he could be at a level above the workbench.

Santa looked up at him and said, "I don't think I have a problem, I know I have a problem!" "Because you think you cannot make enough toys over the next month and a half?"

"Yes," Santa sighed, "that is the problem."

"That should be no problem," continued Clarence, "you don't have to make every toy, do you? Santa slowly shook his head. "All you need is craftsmen to make what you have already designed. Isn't that right?"

Santa nodded his head, "But where am I going to get craftsman up here?" Clarence looked at him with a surprised look on his face, "What do you think these people do up in this part of the world? Everything they have, they made themselves." Santa had not thought of that.

"Do you have the designs?" asked Clarence. Santa nodded yes. "When do you want to get started?" Clarence asked. Santa looked at him wondering what Clarence had in mind. "As soon as possible," replied Santa.

"Good, now you go have lunch. Tell Mrs. Claus to make her specialty stew, pots and pots of it. Also, tell her to start baking her cinnamon buns, as many as she can possibly make. Oh, and I saw a new batch of candy cooling in the kitchen. We will need much more. I will be sending more helpers to her kitchen this afternoon. Now go eat lunch and relax. I will meet you back here in two hours."

Clarence slid off his chair back down to the floor. He looked up at Santa and said, "Don't you worry, the toys will be ready!" He scurried out the door. Clarence saw Hector and Bobbitt working on a project in front of the stables. He quickly went over to them with instructions to rush home and get their wives. Have them come to Mrs. Claus's kitchen immediately. With that Hector and Bobbitt left for home as fast as their little legs could carry them. Clarence met Freddie at the front door of

the house and gave him some instructions that sent him scurrying back into the house. Clarence then headed out of the courtyard, past the little houses and down the road toward his home.

Santa had watched all this activity from his bench as he gazed out through the open doorways. He did not know what Clarence had up his sleeve, but he was slightly relieved with his parting words. Santa pulled the large leather binder in front of him and began to flip through the long list of children and their requests for toys. He could not imagine how he was going to fulfill so many requests. He had this dreadful fear that he was going to disappoint many children this year. He closed the binder and sat back in his chair and sighed. Maybe Clarence does have a plan, he thought. He glanced at his big clock on the wall and realized it was lunchtime. As he walked back to the house, a brisk October breeze reminded him of how close the December 25th deadline was beginning to loom.

Upon entering the house, he could hear the banging of pots and pans coming from the kitchen. When he pushed open the kitchen door he witnessed the most comical scene. There was flour dust flying every- where. Mrs. Claus, Pixie and Suzy and the children were covered from head to toe. Mrs. Claus was making big pots of her specialty stew. Pixie and Suzy were making pie crusts as fast as their little hands could go. The children, standing on the chairs, were rolling out flat sheets of candy on the counter. Poor Freddie was carrying in logs from the wood box and placing them next to the fireplace. Everything was a whirl. But everyone was in a very happy mood. Pixie was whistling and Mrs. Claus was humming as she stirred a big pot of stew. "What's going on here?" Santa called above the activity with merriment in his voice.

"We don't know," Pixie replied, "Clarence told Freddie we needed to have plenty of food ready very quickly."

"And we are helping!" squealed one of the children.

Santa could see he was not going to get any dining room service today. He grabbed a bowl off the shelf and walked over to where Mrs. Claus could ladle out some stew for him. "I will get out of your way," Santa called over his shoulder as he retreated into the dining room. He was pleased that everyone was so happy.

After a few minutes of eating his stew, the front door opened and two more elfin ladies entered. "Hello," one of them said in a gruff voice. "I am Pansy, Hector's wife and this is Tippit, Bobbitt's wife. We were instructed to come and help in the kitchen." Santa pointed toward the kitchen doorway. Both ladies scurried through the door, leaving behind wafts of a flour cloud hanging around the edges of the doorway.

When Santa heard some voices out in the courtyard, he quickly finished his stew and walked out onto the front porch. He could see a line of elfins walking and talking together. They were coming

82

into the courtyard from different directions and walking up the earthen ramp to the workshop. They were all dressed in drab colored apparel with rips and patches, the same as Clarence, Freddie, Hector, and Bobbitt had been wearing when Santa had first discovered them. Santa was watching a procession of workers filing past Clarence at the doorway of the workshop. He waved a hand at Santa when he saw him on the porch. The other arm was cradling a large bowl of candy. Each elfin reached in the bowl and grabbed a large handful of candy as they filed into the workshop. In their other hand, they each carried a small satchel of tools. Even though it was midday, Santa could see the soft glow of light coming through the windows as lanterns were lit inside the buildings.

Santa rushed down the steps and over to Clarence. "Where did you find all these people?" asked Santa, referring to the elves.

"They live throughout the Valley," replied Clarence. "I know them all. They are good carpenters and craftsmen." Clarence turned back to the elfins filing past him, instructing them to grab a handful of candy and then directing them to different areas in the building. Soon, the entire first floor work benches were surrounded with four or five elves. Freddy was distributing toy design drawings that Santa had rolled up in tubes next to his workbench. Other elves were distributing pieces of wood and materials to each of the tables. Soon it could be determined which tables would be making wagons and which would be making rocking horses, while others would be making dolls. There was one table of lady elves sewing small dolls outfits.

Clarence had some of the smaller elves, apparently the children, running back and forth to Mrs. Claus's kitchen, returning with big bowls of candy. Santa's suspicions were correct. Candy would turn the grumpiest of elves into happy elves almost instantly. The more candy they consumed, the louder and happier the sounds of the workers at their workbenches. Clarence and Freddie had everything operating smoothly. Each worker, using the little tools from his satchel, made toys exactly as Santa's directions illustrated. Then the smaller elves would collect completed toys and move them to the painting tables. When the painters were finished, the toys were carried to the drying area. Finally the finished toys were assembled in the large open areas in the middle of the building. The toy pile started to grow. This made Santa feel better, but he knew there would be many long hours of work required to make the number of toys needed.

At the same time, Mrs. Claus's kitchen was beginning to fill up with female elfins. They were all chatting with each other, excitedly, catching up on news as some were making pies, cakes, cinnamon buns and many other delicious treats. Mrs. Claus made sandwiches and her specialty stew. The consistent devouring of candy was also evident in the kitchen area. The more candy eaten, the louder and happier the helpers became. The hustle and bustle of Mrs. Claus's kitchen was more active than she had ever experienced. She loved it. The elfin children continued to pull large pots of hot chocolate from Mrs. Claus's kitchen to Santa's workshop. They were using some of the newly made wagons to pull the pots back and forth. When Mrs. Claus took Santa his special mug of hot chocolate, she was greatly impressed with the organized activity she saw in Santa's workshop. What had previously been a dark dreary building, with Santa's personal workbench near the front door, was now a well-lit large room of activity. Elfins were scurrying everywhere. When she set Santa's tray down next to him on his workbench, he jumped up and hugged her. Swinging his arm about to display the whole room of activity, he excitedly asked, "Isn't this wonderful? I would never have guessed there were so many craftsmen in one area." They both gazed around the room. Mrs. Claus had never seen Santa so happy.

A pile of toys started to build in the center of the floor. Next to the pile of newly built toys, Freddie had Santa's list of children open on a table. He was training some of elfins how to label each toy with a child's name and then would check it off on Santa's list. Santa witnessed, before his very eyes, the efficient manner that Clarence and Freddie had organized his toy making operation. He now felt there would not be a major problem finishing the number of toys needed to fulfill all the children's wishes. This took the weight of the world off Santa's shoulders. He had been so afraid that he might have disappointed many children this coming December 25th.

That is how Clarence and the elves came to Santa's rescue. From that day forward, Santa and Mrs. Claus did everything possible to make the lives of the elves better. Within days, they knew the names of every elf that came to work for them. They knew who was in each family. They made sure each family had everything they needed. In return, the elves did everything they could to return the Clauses' generosity. This, and a constant supply of candy, created one big happy family. The Elfins became known as Elves, and the happy atmosphere began in Santa's workshop that most people are familiar with today.

SANTA'S WORKSHOP

When you think of Santa's workshop, what do you see in your mind? Many people see a vision of Santa in a small workshop with a few toys around him. That is not anything close to the real Santa's workshop. Santa's workshop was initially his little work area inside the great octagonal building on the square.

However, the real definition of Santa's workshop soon became the whole cluster of buildings, Santa's large home, the stables, the large octagonal building, the other work buildings, and the numerous small houses clustered around the little square. As you may recall, when Santa and Mrs. Claus first arrived at their new home, most of the buildings had not been maintained for a number of years. The paint had peeled off most of the buildings, producing a drab, depressing appearance. During the first few weeks, Santa and Mrs. Claus's new found friends were very instrumental in sprucing up the big house and the inside of the work buildings. The first elves the Clauses met, Clarence, Freddie, Hector, Bobbitt and their families, had amazed and surprised Santa. Their fast and spotless cleaning of the house and buildings was completed with remarkable speed.

Santa had quickly moved his tools into the large octagonal building. The area to the right of the big sliding doors was perfect for him. It provided him some privacy, where he could think when he had to do his thinking. Many of his toy ideas came to him when he was in the mood to be thinking. His space also was open enough so he could view the interior area in the octagonal building.

He had a place for his many tools, the saws, hammers, chisels, and other tools for making toys. He also had shelves for the drawings of his toys. His toy design table was very large and many design drawings could be spread on it. His workbench was large and solid.

From his workbench, he had a view of the courtyard if the large sliding doors were open. He also had two large windows with a view of the other two work buildings and any activity in the courtyard in front of his house. The glass in these windows was old. There were little wiggly wavy areas in most of the glass panes. He could also view the whole interior of the octagon building. This building was considered his main workshop.

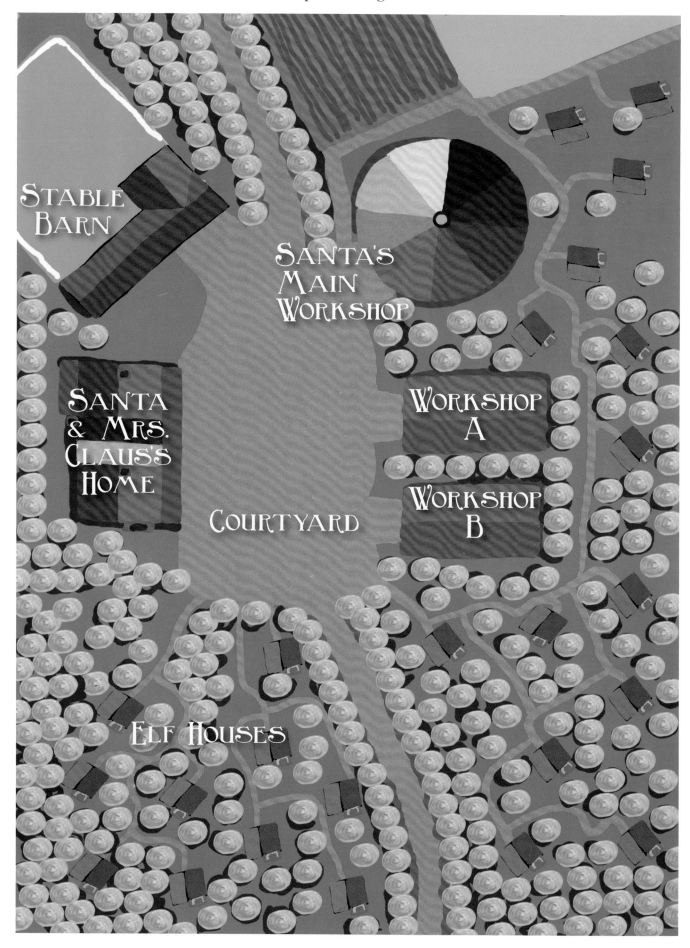

It was a magnificently built building. The three-story walls were made of cobblestone. The heavy wooden planks of the floor had been worn smooth with age. The main floor had two large fireplaces. The previous owners had been wagon builders. The large fireplaces were obviously used by the blacksmiths. When there were fires ablaze in the large fireplaces, they kept the whole building warm and toasty.

There were two balconies, the second floor and the third floor. Each balcony completely circled the inside of the building. Many work tables were on each floor. Large bowls of candy were placed on stands throughout the workshop. This kept the elves very happy. The center of the building had a large planked post. It ran from the center of the main floor up through the center of the roof. It was wide at the bottom and narrowed at the top. A bench had been built around the base of this extremely large pole, making for a resting area for the elves.

The octagonal building and the other two buildings on the courtyard were considered the workshops. However, as mentioned earlier, it was the whole cluster of buildings around the courtyard square that became known as Santa's workshop. That also included the small houses surrounding the work buildings.

Santa's Surprise for the Elves

Neither Santa nor Mrs. Claus paid too much attention to the many small houses just outside the fringe of their little courtyard square. They did not need to. There was no one who needed the little homes. Or so they thought! Many of the great improvements at Santa's workshop area came about by accident. This is exactly how the next great improvement came about for all the small houses.

One day Santa discovered that his supply of wood was going to run out much faster than he anticipated. Clarence assured him there was no problem. After hitching the horses to the wagon, he drove Santa further down the valley to see the type of trees they might need for producing all the toys required. Santa was pleased with the numerous hardwood trees he found in the forests. Upon returning home, he noticed many ugly little shacks scattered throughout the countryside. "What are they used for?" he asked Clarence, pointing to one he could see through the trees. Clarence looked surprised.

"Those are elves' homes," he replied. Santa was dumbfounded. The shacks had holes in the roofs. There were cracks in the walls. The windows had gaps in them. It was apparent the cold air would blow right through these little houses. This disturbed Santa greatly. "Is your house like these?" Santa asked Clarence. "Yes," he replied, "maybe slightly bigger".

"Clarence," Santa asked, "many of the elves are excellent carpenters, why are the homes in such disrepair?"

"There just wasn't time available to repair the homes," replied Clarence. "Most of the time everyone was trying to find food." Santa sat back in the wagon seat, stroking his white beard, as Clarence drove the team back up towards Santa's workshop.

The next day, Clarence found Santa digging through the many cans of paint stored in the paint room. He watched Santa counting cans of one color paint and then writing it down on his little pad. Santa continued this project until he counted the number of cans of each color. He took the pad with all the numbers back to his workbench and sat for many minutes scribbling numbers on the pad.

Clarence was worried.

"Are we running out of paint Santa?" he asked.

"Oh no," Santa assured him, "I have an idea. He motioned Clarence to follow him. As Santa walked towards the big front doors, he motioned for Freddy to come with them also. The three of them walked down the earthen ramp and around the back of the octagon building. They walked through the small spruce trees surrounding the many small vacant houses. Santa stopped in a small clearing, facing the nearest seven or eight little houses. Santa waved his hand toward the houses. "I want you to pick out the one you want," he said to Clarence and Freddie. They both gasped. "Oh Santa, we could not possibly accept your kind offer," they protested. "I am not doing it for you," replied Santa. "I am doing it for me." Both Clarence and Freddie cocked their heads with a quizzical look.

"How long does it take you to walk to the workshop every morning?" Santa asked both of them.

"45 minutes, maybe 50 minutes." They replied.

"I would rather you not have to walk almost two hours a day just to get back and forth. Especially as the days are getting shorter and colder, you would be walking home at night in the dark. "Please, each of you pick out a house. We could make many more toys if you did not have to spend so much time walking back and forth each day. We have enough paint to give them all a fresh coat. I had ordered more paint to be delivered the last time a supply wagon was here." That made sense to the elves.

"Thank you very much Santa. However, may we get Pixie and Suzy? We would like them to be the one to choose." Santa nodded, he understood fully how important it was.

Clarence and Freddie quickly scampered to get their wives, who were working with Mrs. Claus at one of the tables in the great dining hall. They rushed in and frantically motioned to their wives to follow them. Both Pixie and Suzy stood, threw a scarf over their shoulders and followed them out the door. The children came scurrying right behind. The little group walked past the octagon building and through the soft evergreen trees. Freddie explained to Pixie and Suzy what Santa had wanted them to do.

Pixie could not believe her ears. She put her hands up to her face trying to contain her joy. Suzy could not keep from jumping up and down. The children zipped around with the energy of hovering bees. Both Clarence and Freddie were grinning from ear to ear watching the scene of unbridled joy. Pixie and Suzy ran from house to house trying to decide which one would be theirs. Finally, Pixie pointed to the one closest to the courtyard square, which had a full view of Santa's house. Suzy immediately pointed to the one next door to it, squealing, "Freddie, I want that one!" They each rushed into their new homes, flitting around inside exploring every nook and cranny. They

Pixie
&
Clarence

to their Elfinland Inn, they had a completely different outlook of Santa's workshop. They would be consistent and welcomed visitors to the North Pole for many years.

From that time on, Santa's workshop did not refer to merely his bench or the large octagonal building. The whole cluster of buildings and homes nestled down in Hidden Valley at the North Pole was considered Santa's workshop. Unfortunately, the distance to travel to get there was very long.

They did have visitors occasionally, but not nearly as often as they had experienced when living in the North Forest. But that did not matter to them. Now the elves had become their dear friends. Both Santa and Mrs. Claus knew every man, woman, and child elf living at Santa's workshop.

The work areas were constantly alive with activity. The big fireplaces kept everybody warm and toasty. Happy elves would sit around the big center pole during their breaks, eating the many different candies available. Hector and Bobbitt kept the operations in the work areas running smoothly. Clarence and Freddie kept the operations of the whole Santa's workshop community running smoothly. Santa could not have asked for a better group of workers.

Each night, as Santa blew out the candle on his bed stand, he would say to Mrs. Claus, "I hope you are happy. This is a wonderful place to live!" Mrs. Claus would always answer, "I am wonderfully happy, and this is our home!" Within minutes, both would be snoring softly, resting up from a busy day. Unfortunately it would be too dark in the room to see if Santa had placed his beard under the covers or outside the covers.

The Most Famous Candy Invention

When you think of Christmas, what candy do you think of? Many people will say the candy cane. Most homes around the world will have candy canes somewhere in the house. They may be hanging on the tree or be in the candy bowls, or even found in the stockings on Christmas morning. Have you ever wondered where candy canes came from? You may be surprised to discover that candy canes were one of the first inventions that came from Santa's workshop. It is not certain which year they were first developed, but it has a very interesting story. As we know, from the first time they met the elves, Santa and Mrs. Claus discovered how their appearance and attitude improved dramatically when they were fed candy. The very first day of Santa's meeting his first elves, it could be clearly seen how candy greatly improved each elf's appearance. After just a few pieces of candy, their faces transformed from grumpy looking little people into happy, smiley faces with a rosy glow. Their cheeks became fuller, making them look like they were constantly smiling. The truth of the matter is when they could eat as much candy as they wanted, they were constantly smiling. Wouldn't you be?

Santa had also discovered a very unusual feature about elves. After eating candy, the elves seemed to be able to perform tasks in a very unexplainable fashion. They worked at many times the speed that would normally be possible. Candy appeared to have a magical effect on them. Once that was discovered, Mrs. Claus made sure there was a constant supply of candy being made in her kitchen.

Mrs. Claus had a wonderful recipe for a stick candy. It was so simple to make that often the child elves would be responsible for making it. Once it was mixed up, put in the ovens and brought out to cool, the process was very simple. It could be rolled out into very long sticks. As one elf would roll it out, another one would cut it in lengths anywhere from 6 inches to 12 inches long. Once it cooled, the children would put the candy into big baskets that they carried through the workshop areas. The toymaker elves would grab a few sticks as the baskets went by. The baskets were then left near the work tables, always available to everybody.

Who Is Santa?

Santa and Mrs. Claus had discovered the elves were very loyal and trustworthy companions. Once you had shown them generosity, they would return that generosity many-fold. However, the elves had one weak spot. In Hidden Valley, you did not leave your candy unguarded. Leaving your stick candy at your spot at the workbench did not guarantee that your candy would still be there when you got back. Of course, no one at the table would know what happened to it. This meant, if you are stepping away from your spot at the worktable, you took your candy with you. Many candy sticks were shoved in pockets, only to be broken into little bits, which made it difficult for the elves to get their little hands in their pockets to retrieve all the pieces. Of course, it did not really matter as there were plenty of candy baskets throughout the workshop areas. Nobody was ever lacking for candy.

There was also another problem. The sticks of candy were round. Many times they would roll down the table and over the edge, shattering onto the floor, often bringing cries of anguish from different areas of the workshops.

Elves are very creative. If there was a problem, they usually found the right solution. Elf Lucy, a dedicated kitchen worker, came up with a clever idea one day. She knew about the problem of the candy sticks rolling off of things. One day, while she was cutting the candy into twelve-inch lengths, she was thinking about how to keep the candy sticks from rolling off the edges of tables. Suddenly, she had an idea. Around the edges of the counters in the kitchen were many towel bars. She cleared off the towels and started draping the still soft stick candy over the bars.

Mrs. Claus and the other lady elves paused in their kitchen chores and watched Elf Lucy hang many candy sticks over the towel bars. They could not imagine what she was doing. Finally, when the first ones had cooled, Mrs. Claus pulled one off a towel bar. She instantly saw the logic in what Elf Lucy had accomplished. She realized they would now not roll off the tables. "This is a splendid idea," Mrs. Claus said to Lucy. "Candy canes!"

"Watch this!" Lucy exclaimed, as she hooked the candy cane on the front of her apron. "The guys will be able to take their candy with them by just hooking it on their trousers or their work aprons." The other lady elves all clapped with delight as they saw the benefits of a candy cane.

When all the candy had cooled, they loaded the hooked-shaped candy canes into the large baskets. The lady elves took them over to the workshops and passed them out to the work tables. The results were remarkable. You could lay the candy cane down on the table without worrying about it rolling over the edge. But more importantly, the hook on the end made it possible for each elf to take his or her candy cane with them. This greatly impressed the toymakers. All they had to do was throw the hook over their shoulder, on the front of their work aprons or in their belts. They were able to take their candy canes with them wherever they were going. No more worrying about missing candy if you forgot it at your worktable.

was not enough time to check each elf for how each color of candy cane affected their mood and production. After Santa blew out the candle on his bedside table, they both lay there quietly in the dark. "We will find a solution tomorrow." Mrs. Claus said assuredly.

"I hope so," replied Santa.

After a few more moments they were both snoring softly.

ELF LUCY'S GREAT IMAGINATION

Mrs. Claus described the problem to her helpers in the kitchen the next morning. Once again, Elf Lucy came to the rescue. After thinking intently for a few minutes, she finally came up with an idea. She took a hand cranked meat grinder off the end of one of the tables. "I will be right back," she called over her shoulder as she left the kitchen door. She took the meat grinder across the courtyard to her husband, Blinker who was a great tinkerer. He worked in one of the other workshop buildings. Elf Lucy laid the meat grinder down on his table. After describing what she would like, he made a few changes to it and she scurried back to the kitchen. Hooking the converted meat grinder back to the edge of the table, she proceeded to plop a blob of warm, red candy and a blob of warm, white candy in the top of the meat grinder. As she turned the crank, out came a nice smooth flow of candy sticks with the red and the white candy spiraled together. Some of the lady elves immediately cut the strand into twelve-inch lengths. Others would grab the pieces and drape them over the towel bars. When the first large batch was finished, everybody in the kitchen clapped their hands with delight. Each lady elf came over to Lucy and gave her a happy hug. It was a colorful spectacle seeing the spiraled candy canes hanging throughout the kitchen.

The lady elves, the little elves, and Mrs. Claus worked enthusiastically for the next two hours, making the new striped candy canes. They filled up many baskets with the colorful candy. When all the baskets were filled, Mrs. Claus and the lady elves helped load the baskets onto the pull wagons. Excitedly, they helped the little elves pull the wagons across the courtyard to the workshops. They were anxious to see what their husbands and the other workers thought of the new candy canes.

As can be imagined, toy making came to a standstill as the group pulled the wagons into the work areas. It was unusual to have them in the work area, especially unusual to see so many at one time. The little elves put their hands to their mouths and yelled, "new candy, new candy!"

This created a rush to the baskets sitting on the wagons. There were many oohs and aahs as

the toy making elves reached into the baskets and pulled out handfuls of the colorful candy canes. The red and white spirals fascinated the elves. They gobbled down the first ones, and then hung the rest on their suspenders, belts, or caps.

The desire to eat just white canes or red canes immediately disappeared. The striped canes tasted much better, even though the different colored canes were made with exactly the same ingredients. It was very quickly discovered that when these candy canes were distributed throughout the workbenches there were no more symptoms of grumpiness. This was the solution Santa was hoping for. Before the end of the evening, the familiar musical hum was heard once more. This was a very comforting sound to him. As he sat at his workbench, looking out at the work area, he could see all the elves working cheerfully. Everything was good again at Santa's workshop.

Ever since that time, the red and white spiraled candy cane became a favorite of all the elf workers. They soon started appearing in stockings hung on fireplace mantles, extra little treats left by Santa every Christmas. Through the years, the tasty treat of a candy cane has become a favorite of many children around the world.

THE POLE

As late December drew near, the arctic winds brought temperatures down dramatically. Santa's workshop felt the cold. There were two large fireplaces in the octagonal building. The roaring flames were constantly kept fed with an endless supply of logs. These fireplaces were very large, keeping the workshop area well lit. The other two work buildings also had two large fireplaces each. Each day grew darker earlier and much colder and the effects could be felt by everybody at the North Pole. Especially in the late afternoons, the temperatures would drop. Even with the fires roaring and the lanterns ablaze, the darkness was noticed in the back of the work area. Even so, there was little change in the work atmosphere for the happy attitude of all the elves made the work areas light and cheerful.

One afternoon, as Santa, Clarence, and Freddie were having a hot chocolate break at his workbench, Santa mentioned that their next project would be to find a way to make the octagonal workshop have more working light inside. Even with the roaring fires and brightly lit lanterns hanging above the work tables, it was still slightly dark, especially on those dark, cloudy, snowy afternoons. Both Clarence and Freddie looked at Santa somewhat quizzically. "What?" Santa inquired, looking back and forth at each one of them, wondering why the elves appeared as if that suggestion was unusual.

Clarence pointed to the center of the building, and said "The pole."

"Hanging lights on the center pole?" questioned Santa. He thought to himself, that wouldn't add much more light.

"No, the pole." stated Clarence still pointing to the big center column in the middle of the building holding up the roof. Santa did not understand. In the very center of the octagon shaped building was a large pole structure that had wooden boards covering it from the floor up through the ceiling. Santa had always assumed the design of the building required the big center pole to hold up the roof. The steeple protruding through the top of the roof provided a bluish glow that made an excellent marker for trying to find Santa's workshop at night. The glowing steeple could be seen for many miles around. It was not a bright glow, just a soft pleasant blue shade of light that could be

107

seen from great distances. The round base of the pole was approximately six feet across at the floor. It slowly tapered up to approximately a foot and a half across at the ceiling. A sitting bench had been built approximately eighteen inches off the floor around the base and was a popular gathering place for the elves to sit and eat cookies and drink hot chocolate during their breaks.

The wooden vertical boards were well fitted to the taper of the pole as it got narrower near the top. Santa never paid too much attention to the center structure, he just thought it was the way it was built to hold up the roof! There was a constant clamor of chatter and laughter at the meeting place around the pole. Tables close by had pots of hot chocolate and hot cider and many large baskets of candy, muffins and cookies on other tables nearby. This was a popular place for the elves to chat and visit with each other during their rest breaks. The vertical planks were used as a message board. Notices would usually be tacked on it for all to read, such as "Whoever put marshmallows on my chair, please stop. I was stuck to my chair for two hours yesterday." The elves were a happy and jolly bunch with an air of fun and mischievousness always present.

"The pole," Clarence repeated, clearly seeing that Santa did not understand. "The North Pole!" Clarence got up from his seat and pulled a large pry bar from one of Santa's toolboxes. He strolled over to the center pole. It took him a moment to find a seam to get the edge of the pry bar placed between the boards. With a mighty shove, one of the boards creaked loudly but only moved slightly. Another elf stepped up and helped Clarence push on the pry bar. Again, the planks creaked and started separating slightly. Another hard push brought one of the planks slightly away from the other planks. A warm glow emitted from behind the plank. Another hard shove on the pry bar popped one of the major boards off of the pole. It rattled loudly onto the floor. The area was now aglow with a nice yellow colored light shining in the blank space.

At this point, work came to an absolute standstill. Every elf in the building had turned their eyes toward the center pole. Many had gathered around watching the activity. The balcony railings were lined with elves as well. Soon, more elves helped remove planks. Underneath was what appeared to be a solid pole of the ice. It glowed with a very warm color of yellow. As the first layer of the wooden planks were taken off, those above slowly started sliding down the pole, separating slowly as they slid. By now, a dozen elves were grabbing the boards as they were coming down the pole. Soon the whole pole was exposed! A massive column of ice, coming up through the floor of the building and protruding up through the roof, produced a warm yellow glow at the bottom and slowly turned into a warm blue color as it went out through the roof. The light from the pole lit up every nook and cranny in the large octagon building. Santa was amazed! He rushed over and touched it. It was cold to the touch but it did not give off any cold.

"Run, get Mrs. Claus immediately!" he yelled to some of the elves by the door.

They scampered across the courtyard and up the steps into the house. "Mrs. Claus, Mrs. Claus and everybody, come quick!" they yelled. The lady elves came rushing out of the kitchen.

Mrs. Claus put down her work and immediately went out the front door. The large contingency of lady elves and Mrs. Claus could see a strong warm glow projecting through the windows and the open front door of the main workshop.

They hurried across the courtyard and into the building to find a great glowing column of ice. "What is it?" Mrs. Claus exclaimed.

"Ho Ho Ho! Mama, we are at the North Pole." He turned to Clarence, "Why didn't you tell me the North Pole was right here?"

"I thought you knew," replied Clarence. "The wagon makers were not impressed. They covered it up and then built the octagonal building around it. I just assumed big people did not have any appreciation for the North Pole."

The lady elves filled the entire front door entrance as they gazed at the pole. Every worker in the building was at the railings gazing happily at the pole. We already know that Santa had his special magic powers. It was apparent that the elves had their own magic powers. It can also be assumed that a natural wonder like the North Pole had its own magic powers, too.

Once the pole was fully exposed with all the wooden planks removed, the lighting was much more abundant, filling the whole building with a warm glow. Every elf in the building was clapping happily. The elves working in the other buildings came rushing across the courtyard and crowded into the octagonal workshop building to see what the commotion was. Everyone began to clap gleefully when they saw the pole glowing in the center of the building! A celebration of the pole included many shared pots of hot chocolate as everyone stood and marveled at the beloved landmark. It's magic could be felt by everybody, a magical feeling that spread through the crowd. The rest of the day had a festive atmosphere. As the sun began to set, very large snowflakes started to fall. Clarence remarked that this was the first time in many years the snow fall was nice, quiet flakes rather than the gusty, stinging, cold, wind-blown snow. The large snowflakes reflecting the warm light protruding through the windows gave Santa's workshop a very cozy and Christmassy atmosphere.

All the powers of the North Pole cannot be specifically scientifically documented, but the following spring, it was noticed that cinnamon trees and marshmallows bushes were sprouting in the area. These had not been seen growing in Hidden Valley for many years.

Although the cluster of buildings, known as Santa's workshop, was surrounded by evergreen trees, a warm and friendly glow of light could be seen above the trees for many miles around. Santa and Mrs. Claus felt very proud knowing they had established Santa's workshop at the top of the world, the true North Pole.

THE FIRST NORTH POLE CHRISTMAS

Many years prior to arriving at the North Pole, Santa and Mrs. Claus had gone through the unique experience of delivering toys late at night throughout the North Forest region. She could clearly remember the anxiety she went through that first night as Santa and the men from the farm went out into the darkness to deliver toys to hundreds of children. Mrs. Claus could also remember the fear of what might happen to them in the darkness. There was a doubt that the slow lumbering wagons could travel hundreds and hundreds of miles in just one night. Although she had had her doubts and worries, somehow, Santa Claus was able to fulfill that task. Mrs. Claus never asked, specifically, how it was completed, but she just knew the magic Santa had for making people happy would somehow make things work.

Now many years later, there were those same fears and doubts as the first Christmas from the North Pole was approaching. Santa's first concerns were about the quality of the toys the elves were making with great speed. It turned out though that there were very few mistakes or problems. Santa was very pleased with the quality of work of his elf helpers. Mrs. Claus was greatly concerned that Santa was going to travel out into the night. This time he would have only one wagon, but many more toys than that first night in the North Forest as well as a much greater distance that needed to be traveled. However, the one thing that she had learned throughout the years was when Santa said he was able to do something, he was able to do it, and she trusted what he said.

As December 25th grew closer and closer, the activity at Santa's workshop became more frenzied. The elves checked Santa's wish list with the name tags on the toys. The horses were groomed each day, and they were well fed and strengthened for the trip. Mrs. Claus made sure a large pot of Santa's favorite hot chocolate would be ready to put underneath the wagon seat.

Even Clarence had his concerns about how they were going to get all the toys into one large wagon. Just looking at the piles of toys, now stacked in the center of the main workshop and the two other work buildings, it was obviously many hundreds of times more than Santa's one wagon. But Clarence rationalized, just like Mrs. Claus, if Santa was not concerned, then he was not going to be concerned. This attitude was somewhat the result of knowing there were certain things magic would take care of. Even elves had their own magical traits!

Christmas Night

Once again Christmas Eve had arrived. Mrs. Claus pulled out a new Santa suit for the occasion. Any doubts about him being able to deliver the multitude of toys had disappeared. Even Clarence's momentary uncertainty disappeared after the arrival of the latest shipment of supplies. As it rumbled slowly into the courtyard, Santa came running out to greet the driver. He was anxious to hear any news from the outside world. He asked the driver how his friends, Ivan and Ingrid, were doing. The driver assured Santa they were doing well. He then handed over a packet of letters. They were from his friends back in the North Forest. Most importantly, Santa quickly pawed through the supplies and found a special package of material. He then instructed the driver to unload everything over in one of the work buildings. He bounded up the front steps and gave the packet of letters to Mrs. Claus.

Santa quickly opened the package of material he had under his arm. It was a soft leathery material. He quickly strolled over to the other work building. He laid out the material in front of Hickey, an elf with special sewing skills. Santa showed him how he would like a carrying sack to be put together for carrying the toys. Later that day, Hickey brought the finished sack over to Santa's workbench. "Excellent!" cried Santa. "This should do the trick." After stretching it one way and then the other, he was anxious to give it a try. He called for Hector, who had been put in charge of stacking the finished toys. He came over to Santa's bench and Santa handed him the sack. "Start filling the sack with the toys," he instructed Hector. He watched as Hector and several other elves began putting toys into the sack. He was pleased when he saw the large quantity of toys that seemed to fill the sack. But it did not stop there . . . nothing seemed to stop its ability to continue to take more toys! Santa knew he would be able to get all his toys into it. Clarence had also been watching this process. He was greatly relieved to see that no matter how many toys were put into the sack, it did not seem to fill up to the brim! Satisfied, Hector went back to his other projects of getting Santa prepared for Christmas Eve.

Finally, the night everybody was waiting for arrived. There were light snowflakes falling as

Santa stepped out onto the front porch that evening. He looked as proud as a peacock in his new red suit, trimmed with white furry cuffs and black belt and buttons. Every elf at Santa's workshop was crowded onto the front porch and around the wagon, standing ready in front of the porch. The racket intensified through the crowd as the elves complimented Santa on his beautiful outfit. There were many oohs and aahs. Mrs. Claus had brought out a big pot of hot chocolate. One of the elves put it under the wagon seat. She also had a basket full of honey buns, muffins, candy and cookies to go along with it. Soon, it came time for Santa to start his long Christmas Eve journey. At the top of the steps, he spread his arms wide open, facing all the eager faces of his elf friends. "I cannot thank you enough, my good friends. You have made this year's journey a success." All of the elves clapped and cheered. Santa gave Mrs. Claus a big hug and a kiss. He then turned to Clarence, put his hand on Clarence's shoulder and asked, "What would you think about coming with me tonight?" Clarence's eyes grew wide as saucers, "Do you mean it Santa? I would be honored to ride with you tonight." With that, the elves clapped and cheered again. Pixie immediately handed Clarence a heavier coat. She wrapped a heavy scarf around his neck. Then she straightened his cap, which immediately slid back to a funny angle on his head. She gave him a kiss on his cheek. His children hugged his legs, then raised their palms up, wiggling their fingers, which was their way of getting him to bend down for a kiss goodbye.

Clarence and Santa then climbed aboard the wagon. Before Santa sat down, he raised one of his white furry gloves in the air, "Ho Ho Ho!," he laughed waving to all the elves and Mrs. Claus. "Ho Ho Ho!," responded many of the elves, but in much higher and squeakier voices. Clarence snapped the reins lightly as the large workhorses slowly pulled away from the crowd of elves in the courtyard. They continued to wave and follow the wagon, with the pleasant yellow glow of the North Pole at their backs. The glow illuminated Santa and the wagon until it left the courtyard square, through the evergreen trees, on the road up and out of Hidden Valley. The first Christmas from the North Pole had just begun.

SANTA'S SLEIGH

Many of the improvements for making more toys at the North Pole came from careful planning, along with a method to get the toys to children around the world. Other improvements occurred by accident and occasionally some were the result of misunderstandings that turned out good. Santa's sleigh was one of those situations. Santa and Mrs. Claus were always generous to the elves and the elves returned the same generosity to the Clauses. This made the working atmosphere at Santa's workshop very pleasant throughout the year. However, there would occasionally be a miscommunication or some grumpiness developing. This was usually the result of one of the elves not getting enough candy.

The elves worked hard throughout the year, knowing the massive amounts of toys required for each Christmas Eve. This meant things needed to be orderly and run smoothly. A glitch in the operations could affect the number of toys produced. A goof up at the carving or assembly table would disrupt the number of toys that needed to go to the painting table, and so on. Fortunately, the elves had very efficient methods and the elves enjoyed their work. There was often much whistling and humming coming from the many work tables in Santa's workshops. It was common practice for the elves to help each other to make sure the supply of finished toys remained on schedule. There was a genuine thoughtfulness from each elf towards the other elves and the Clauses.

This genuine thoughtfulness unfortunately created one of the most well-known misunderstandings ever to occur at the North Pole. It occurred during the year after Santa's first trip from the North Pole. As you may recall, Santa and Clarence set off on Christmas Eve with the crowd of elves waving goodbye. They rumbled out of the courtyard square in the big wagon pulled by the team of powerful horses. Obviously, there were some concerns because the number of children on Santa's list had grown. Mrs. Claus and the rest of the elves spent a restless night waiting for them to return. As daylight just started to break on the horizon, the jingling of the wagon's bells could be heard as they came down the road, then through the evergreen trees, and back into the courtyard square. As you can imagine, Mrs. Claus and all the elves were waiting anxiously. They all cheered as they heard Santa's "Ho Ho Ho!" just before the wagon entered the courtyard. As the horses and wagon appeared, all the elves ran forward to greet the wagon. They were dancing and laughing as they followed the wagon up to the front steps of Santa's house. He jumped down and gave Mrs. Claus a big kiss as the elves crowded around. "Another successful trip," he announced. "We delivered exactly the right amount of toys to everybody on the list." Clarence had reached into the back of the wagon and held up the empty sack. All the elves were jumping up and down excitedly, clapping their hands.

Santa reached under the wagon seat. He pulled out a leather bound book and held it in the air. "We have a list for the next year!" The elves once again cheered and clapped. Then they wandered back to the work- shop buildings to get ready to make the next round of toys. A few of the elves remained with Santa and Mrs. Claus. Norman was one of the elves who stayed behind. He carried the empty pot of hot chocolate back into the kitchen. Santa and Clarence sat down at the big dining table and had a hearty breakfast.

"Tell us about the trip," begged one of Clarence's children. The small group of elves listened intently as Santa and Clarence described the evening. "Because the list was so much bigger this year," Santa said, "the time seemed to go much more slowly. We got to everybody on the list, but it was much more difficult. First, because we are so far north, it took a long time just to travel to the areas where we needed to start delivering toys. The horses did a very good job getting us through the initial part of the trip, just getting back down to the Elfinland Inn took quite a bit of time. Clarence chimed in, "The winds were howling once we got out of Hidden Valley. The snow was swirling so bad, we had great difficulty seeing more than a few feet in front of us."

"Yes," Santa added, "the horses did a very good job in staying on the right course, but it was much more difficult than last year." Both Santa and Clarence looked totally exhausted. They could barely keep their eyes open as they were eating breakfast and describing the trip. "I am very concerned that we might have reached the limit of our powers to deliver that many toys in just one night." Obviously, his reference to their powers was probably referring to the use of his magic powers. Clarence, in a state of exhaustion, nodded in agreement. After describing the plights of traveling that far in one night, to the small group of elves listening intently in the dining room, Santa and Clarence headed each to their beds. Both of them slept soundly through the day and all the way until sunrise the next morning.

Norman had been listening to their stories. He was very concerned about Santa's worries of not being able to get to more children the next year. The elves had found a very happy and comfortable working atmosphere in Santa's workshop. If they could not accommodate new children on the list for

next year, that might bring a wonderful tradition of delivering toys at night to a standstill. Everybody knew about Santa's great despair period this past year when he thought he could not deliver to all the children on the list. Elves have a great tendency to be affected by the moods of those around them. What if Santa had a longer list next year and really thought he could not deliver toys to them? Do you think he would be down hearted and maybe even a little depressed? If the whole elf workforce started feeling the effects of Santa being downtrodden, it could affect the entire elves' attitude. No amount of candy would be able to help. This just could not be allowed to happen!

Norman took it upon himself to see if he could come up with a solution. The problem was not so much about whether the elves could produce enough toys, but whether all those toys could be delivered. This put Norman into a great thinking mode. He had to come up with an idea that would help Santa be able to get to more children on Christmas Eve. He knew the solution was not going to be easy. He suspected Santa was at the limit of his magical powers to be able to deliver as many toys as he could now. Although nothing was ever mentioned about magical powers, most of the elves took it for granted that Santa had some very strong magical powers. They could see there were many things that Santa could get done that were not explainable. This was no major concern to many of the elves. Every elf seemed to have some degree of magical powers themselves. They would use those powers for performing some of the tasks they did. For example, Hickey was able to sew together a sack for Santa that could carry a huge abundance of toys, much more than would normally be scientifically or physically possible. Other elves also appeared to have magical powers when making toys. Many had skills that allowed them to make toys much faster than normally possible.

Norman's main responsibility was taking care of the animals at Santa's Workshop. He possessed an unusual and rare power to be able to talk to and understand the animals. The workhorses had developed a great fondness to him. There were also reindeer under his care, as well as sheep and goats. The fenced pasture behind Santa's house was large enough to allow them all to run together. Norman enjoyed taking care of the animals. Care of feeding them and keeping the stable barn clean was a major portion of his responsibilities. It gave him a lot of time to think. This is what he did for many hours, days, and weeks after he listened to Santa's concerns the morning he returned from delivering presents from the first North Pole Christmas.

Norman pondered the problem of how to move the big wagon faster. Something had to be done about the speed in which Santa could move around on Christmas night. More horses? No, that would not work. They would all still move together at the same speed. Maybe some magic food for the horses that might make them move much faster. That was possible, however Norman could not think of any of the elves working at the North Pole who might have magic for the animals' feed. If anybody would have that magic, it would be Norman, and he already knew he didn't have anything like that.

Days passed and Norman continued to think about how to solve Santa's problem. Now Norman had a knack and was really good at fixing problems. Elves often brought toys they were working on to Santa's personal workbench. They would describe an idea recommended by Norman for improving a toy. Quite often, Santa agreed and gave his approval. Soon Santa and Clarence were aware of Norman's talents for seeing how to improve toys. Occasionally, they would call on Norman from the stable barn. He would join them at Santa's workbench whenever there was a problem with a toy design that Santa could not solve. Sometimes, after a few minutes, Norman would make a suggestion that seemed to solve the problem. Other times, Norman would carry the problem around in his head for a few weeks. As he cared for the animals, he would be constantly trying to figure out how an answer to one of Santa's design problems. More often than not he eventually came up with a solution.

This did not make Norman any wiser or smarter than any of the other elves. It was just his special talent. He could not whittle or carve like the some of the elves. He could not paint very expressive faces on dolls like other elves, and he realized each of us have a special knack or gift. His gift seemed to be problem solving. Although he had come up with many good ideas during the year he still could not come up with a way to move Santa faster and to more houses on Christmas Eve.

As it was getting later into the year, Norman was pondering that very problem one morning. Everybody knew there were some concerns about whether Santa would be able to make the trip all in one night this coming Christmas Eve and Santa could be heard expressing some doubts. Clarence and Freddie would often try to come back with positive responses. They knew what might happen to the workers' morale if it had gotten out that Santa did not think he could deliver to all the children in one night. Clarence had learned that when the pressure to get all the toys done began to affect Santa Claus, he could have moments of grumpiness. Yes, even Santa had a moment of grumpiness!

Clarence knew to immediately find Mrs. Claus. She was always able to diffuse Santa's grumpy nature pretty quickly.

NORMAN'S BIG IDEA

Norman started formulating a new solution for Santa one day as he was sitting on the pasture fence taking a break. As he was watching the animals, a small herd of reindeer caught his attention. The horses, sheep, and goats were usually standing still, as they were grazing. The reindeer, however, almost always ran in a pack at the far end of the pasture. Watching them from a great distance, Norman marveled at how it seemed like they were floating or even flying as they pranced back-and-forth way down at the lower end of the pasture. Flying, thought Norman …now that would be a much faster way for Santa to get from house to house. The light started to come on in Norman's head. Flying? How could I teach the reindeer to fly?

This started a major thinking process for Norman. Now most people realize they cannot teach animals how to fly, but we know Norman had some magical powers he could draw upon to even attempt such a thing. For the next few weeks, Norman could be seen working with the small herd of reindeer at the far end of the pasture.l

Norman knew he had not completely resolved Santa's problem. Even if he could make reindeer fly, they were obviously not strong enough to pull the heavy wagon, let alone get it off the ground. Although this could be a big problem, he continued to work with the reindeer. It was not until a few weeks later when he was cleaning out a large back room in the stable barn that "Presto!" the problem was solved.

That back room was filled with old farm equipment and parts. The sheep flock was getting bigger since there had been many babies added to the flock this past spring. Norman knew he would have to find more space in the stable barn. He wanted to make sure the sheep had more warm space available before the cold winter months arrived.

As he was cleaning out the farm equipment room, in the very back he came across an elegant sleigh. Even in its broken-down condition, Norman could see that at one time it had been a very high quality, well-built snow sleigh. The front seat and the back seat were well cushioned. As it stood, some of the upholstery was ripped and the thin wood paneling on the sides was broken. One of the snow runners underneath was broken in two places. This made the sleigh unusable in its current state. Norman suspected that was why it had been put away in the back of this room. He found other elves to help him move the farm equipment and parts to an outside shed. But he kept the old sleigh just inside the door, making it the only thing left in the room. He had an idea forming in his head. He did not have it completely thought out yet, but he knew he should keep the sleigh where he could see it.

As the weeks continued, the next Christmas Eve was getting closer and closer. Santa's friend, Ivan, from the Elfinland Inn, had made another visit recently. Santa and Mrs. Claus were very pleased to see him. They asked about his wife, Ingrid, and his daughter, Eva. He reported they were both in good health and made sure to send the Clauses their best wishes. Ivan had a pleasant stay, eating and telling stories of the far North to the Clauses and many of the elves, while enjoying the warmth of the dining room fireplace. Although the visit from Ivan was enjoyed by all, there was one bad result. Ivan had brought three large sacks of letters from children requesting toys from Santa Claus. This was over and above what Santa already had on his list.

This created more pressure in the workshops. Although Santa was concerned, he knew they could get the work done. Mrs. Claus and her kitchen helpers made sure there was a constant supply of candy, cookies, muffins and pie available to Santa's helpers. The hot chocolate pots were constantly being refilled and there was an abundance of marshmallows to add to the hot chocolate. Once the actual North Pole had been uncovered, the cinnamon trees and marshmallow bushes started to sprout up abundantly in the springtime.

Norman was oblivious to Santa's new problems. He was working on resolving Santa's travel problems. The progress he was making in teaching the reindeer how to fly was very impressive, even to Norman himself.

One day, as the reindeer were demonstrating they could fly, and fly with no limits, the idea suddenly came to Norman. What if the reindeer were hooked up to a much lighter vehicle such as the sleigh that was in the barn? This really excited Norman! He quickly waved the reindeer back to the ground. They had been flying up overhead as he was standing in the lower part of the pasture. As they landed, the reindeer understood that he wanted them to stay down and graze. He bounded back up the pasture as fast as his little legs would take him. He threw open the door to the back room and inspected the sleigh from top to bottom. He made a quick list: repair the upholstery and the wooden sides, rebuild the sleigh runner, replace the leather harness pieces, and repaint the sleigh.

He immediately went to work repairing the sleigh. Hickey, the elf in charge of sewing and materials, gave him what he needed to repair the upholstery. However, he had difficulty once it came

to getting the rest of the materials. These he would have to obtain through Clarence or Freddie, but when he tried to ask them for materials, both of them said to come back later, they were busy right then. Certainly they were busy! Suddenly, with the arrival of the three large bags of letters a few weeks before Christmas, the number of toys needed this year had dramatically increased. These letters were from new children who had learned that Santa delivered toys each year. Clarence and Freddie were working in a frenzy to meet their new demand.

They had to call in some of the outside elves. These are elves that did not normally work with toy making. Some elf crews would take the heavy wagon into the forest and chop down trees. The trees were used for lumber, both for building additional little houses around Santa's Workshop Square and for supplying wood for the manufacturing of the toys. Other elf crews were responsible for maintaining the supply of firewood. They would be chopping and stacking wood most of the day. Some elves were in charge of harvesting cinnamon from the cinnamon trees in the forest, or collecting marshmallows from the marshmallow bushes. All these elves were now recruited to help with the making of toys. This made Clarence and Freddie even busier than they had ever been before. It was a very intricate process to coordinate new workers with their supply of materials. Hector and Bobbitt, in charge of materials distribution, worked diligently to make sure all the right supplies went to the right worktables at the right time.

It was during this frenzied time that Norman stood in the center of the octagonal building, looking all around him, watching all the activity. Sometimes he wished he was more a part of this work area, but he also knew his job was very important, taking care of the animals.

Norman did not want to disturb the well-oiled workshop process he could see in operation. He did not want to disturb Clarence or Hector or Bobbitt. He could see they were working very hard. Norman knew what he needed and he knew where everything was in storage. He went to the wood supply room and picked up the sheets of wood he would need to repair the sleigh. With them under his arm he gaily waved to some of his friends as he left the big workshop. Nobody would have taken notice of it except for a number of observations that came together all at one time.

During the previous few nights, when Santa and Mrs. Claus were getting ready for bed, Santa was telling Mrs. Claus how concerned he was they may not be able to get all the toys finished in time for Christmas Eve. Mrs. Claus reassured him everything would be fine. She knew Clarence had made plans to bring in some of the outside elf crews to help with the year-end toy building. Trying to be helpful, she mentioned that it might be helpful to have the other elves with less pressing duties come into the workshops and help with building toys. "What do you mean?" Santa inquired. Mrs. Claus explained how she had come out on the back kitchen porch a few times and noticed Norman way

down in the pasture. He was teaching the reindeer how to fly.

"Teaching the reindeer how to fly?" Santa bellowed. This really irritated him because he knew how hard all the other elves had been working. "Teaching the reindeer how to fly? How ridiculous!" Although Norman had helped many times in solving workshop problems, all Santa could think about right then was getting all the toys finished before Christmas Eve. This was the most important thing on his mind. Having an elf goofing off when his help would be needed was just frustrating!

Norman Makes Santa Mad

The big blowup did not occur until a few days later. After Norman had replaced the broken wood on the sides of the sleigh, he went back to the supply rooms and pulled out a few long strips of flat metal pieces. These were used to make the metal wheels on the baby carriages. They worked perfectly for making new runners on the sleigh. He got a can of red paint and finished putting a new coat of paint on the outside of the sleigh. He repaired the upholstery and oiled it to make it nice and soft. It was on his final trip to the supply rooms when the problems finally hit.

As described before, the production lines in Santa's workshops were very well coordinated. All the right materials would arrive at the right tables at the right time. A malfunction would slow down the whole process. The right piece of wood not getting to the wagon makers would mean the wagon would be held up. That would hold up the painters, which would then hold up the elves taking products to the drying racks. When everything was running smoothly, there was a merry hum in the workshops. Santa, Clarence, and Freddie, as well as the rest of the workshop could tell when production was out of whack. The sound of the work from a specific area would turn into a whining high pitched sound. The squeaky voices of panicky workers could be heard, changing the tone of the room in that area.

When this occurred, Clarence knew immediately to get to that area and find out what was missing. First, some pieces of wood had not arrived at the wagon workbench and the dollhouse workbench. He sent elves running over to the other two work building supply rooms to find replacement pieces. However, during that time the rest of the process could be heard slowing down. Not too long after that, a whining sound could be heard over on the baby carriage workbenches. Pieces of the metal wheel rims had not gotten to them. They had baby carriages now piling up on their bench because they were not able to finish. Things started getting really bad when the slow-down noise was heard over in the paint area. By this time, it was becoming evident there were severe problems occurring. Santa looked up from his workbench when he heard the tone of the room changing. He got up and

went out onto the center of the floor. "What's wrong?" he yelled over to Clarence. "There seems to be some material missing," replied Clarence. This really distressed Santa because he knew how crucial it was to keep the toy production going as fast as possible to make this year's deadline. Unfortunately for Norman, this was the time that he had just picked up a small can of black paint to finish the touch-ups on the elegant sleigh he had been working on for Santa. He had the misfortune of walking by a disgruntled Santa at that very moment. Santa noticed a can of paint in Norman's hand. "Where did you get that?" Santa bellowed at Norman. Norman stopped in his tracks. The whole workroom came to an immediate stop. Nobody had ever heard Santa speak with that harsh a tone. Clarence and Freddie had an instant fear run through them. They knew Santa was under great pressure. He could do or say something that might affect the mood of the whole workshop. Unfortunately, they were both too far away to prevent what happened next.

"From the supply room," answer Norman in a meek voice. He did not understand why Santa had questioned him so harshly.

"You have affected our whole toy making process," Santa yelled. "Get out, and do not come back in here again." This completely stunned poor Norman. He stood there and looked at Santa with tears welling up in his eyes. He did not understand what he had done. He was not familiar with the supply system in the workshop. Every elf in the building watched in silent horror. Elves had rushed to the railings on the upper balconies. They had never seen or heard Santa yell at anybody. Clarence rushed back over as quickly as he could, but the damage was done. Norman quickly ran from the building and back to the stable barn. There was a dreadful silence that followed.

Clarence and Freddie each took Santa by the arm and walked him back to his workbench. Santa all of a sudden felt very badly. He had never yelled at anybody before.

"All right," Clarence yelled stepping back out onto the middle of the floor, "everybody back to work. We will have the supply problem taken care of in the next few minutes." The elves turned back to their tables to work but it took awhile for the familiar, friendly hum to build back up in the workshop.

Norman did not know what he had done. He thought he was doing a very nice thing for Santa, trying to find a way that he would not be so exhausted at the end of his Christmas night trip. Now Norman was at the bottom of the world. He had tears flowing from his eyes when he got back to the stable barn. Some of the animals had come back to their stalls because it was nearing dusk. They watched Norman stumble into the barn and rush past them. That was not normal. Usually Norman would pet and talk to each one of them as they came back in for the evening.

Something was terribly wrong tonight. Norman was looking for some place to hide. He opened the door to the back room where the nice, big, elegant sleigh was sitting. He climbed up onto the back seat and curled himself up and cried for a very long time. Santa did not know what to do. Clarence and Freddie kept assuring him they would find Norman and make things right. However, they could not find Norman in the stable barn. They did not know about the back room area. Santa noticed the cheery waves of goodbye from the elves leaving for the evening did not seem to have the same flourish as usual.

"Oh, what have I done?" thought Santa. As usual, in situations like this, it was Mrs. Claus who came to the rescue. Of course the news had reached the kitchen very quickly, which was usual for anything that happened at Santa's workshop. When Mrs. Claus heard what happened, she rushed over to Santa's workbench. He looked at her as she approached with her usual mug of hot chocolate and gingerbread cookie. She could tell by his eyes that he felt very bad. She came around his workbench, laid the tray of hot chocolate and cookies in front of him, gave him a reassuring hug and said, "Everything is going to be all right." His shoulders slumped. "I hope you're right," he replied. She patted him on the back and then headed for the stable barn.

It was dark when she went inside the stable barn. She was not very familiar with this barn. There was really no need for her to enter it. She had only been inside once or twice since they moved to their new home. She lit several of the lanterns hanging on the big square posts. The glow of the lanterns allowed her to see some of the horses and reindeer sticking their heads out of their stalls. She yelled Norman's name several times, getting no reply. She picked up one of the lanterns as she walked along the stalls toward the other end of the barn. Norman was nowhere to be seen. She noticed one last door. When she opened it, the light from her lantern lit up a fairly large room with stone walls. It was clean and empty, other than a sleigh sitting near a large sliding door that led to the outside. "Norman," she called. No answer, however she heard a slight squeak coming from the sleigh. She walked over and found Norman curled up in a little ball sitting on the back seat. "Oh Norman," she said quietly as he looked up at her with big tear-filled eyes. She climbed up into the back of the sleigh, sat on the back seat and put her arms around the elf.

He put his little arms around Mrs. Claus and cried, "I don't know what I did to make Santa so mad at me." Mrs. Claus hugged him tighter. "I was just trying to help," he continued with his little trembling voice.

"You did nothing wrong," Mrs. Claus answered him. "Santa is just greatly worried that all the toys will not be ready this year. You know all the toys need to be ready for Christmas Eve next week." She could feel Norman nodding his head against her as she was holding him tightly. "You just happened to be at the wrong place at the wrong time. You know Santa loves you and all the elves here?" Again, she felt Norman's head nodding against her side as she held him. They both sat there in the back of the sleigh for quite a few minutes. The small lantern produced a pool of light around the sleigh but did not reach the dark walls of the room.

"Mama? Norman?" they heard Santa calling from the front part of the stable barn.

"In here," answered Mrs. Claus. "Where?" replied Santa. "In the back room, down past the stalls." In a few moments, they heard the creak of the door as Santa came into the room. He saw the little pool of light around the sleigh. "Is Norman with you?" he asked as he could not see Norman's head above the back of the sleigh seat. He saw her nod her head as he approached the sleigh.

"Oh Norman, I am so sorry that I yelled at you." Santa felt even worse when he saw Norman's tear-filled eyes look up at him. "Will you ever forgive me?" Santa asked. "I should never have yelled at you, my good friend."

A look of happiness came into Norman eyes. He reached his arms up to give Santa a hug. Santa hugged him back. "I did not know what I did to make you so mad." He said to Santa. "I just wanted to have your sleigh all fixed up for you." Santa looked at the sleigh. "Oh yes, what a fine job you have done. The sleigh looks superb." In actuality, Santa did not understand what Norman was trying to convey. He did not want to hurt Norman's feelings by mentioning the sleigh looked very nice, but there were many more important things to be doing right now.

"Are you hungry?" Norman nodded his head. "Why don't you come eat dinner with me? I heard that Mrs. Claus has a splendid dinner ready." Norman climbed down from the sleigh, Santa helping Mrs. Claus down right behind him. They each took one of Norman's hands and walked back to the main house and had a nice dinner together. Life was good again.

That evening, as Santa and Mrs. Claus were getting into bed, she made some very pointed reminders for Santa. She described to him how the elves looked up to Santa. He had been kind to them from the very beginning. He had moved them from cold drafty hovels across the Valley into nice, warm, solid houses. They loved to work for him because he treated everybody well. They had plenty of food and candy. She reminded him that if he made any one of them unwanted, it would be like threatening them to be going back to their existing lifestyle before the Clauses had arrived. They both knew every elf at the North Pole. They were all like family. "Next time," she wagged her finger at him, "if you feel the urge to yell at somebody, count to ten first." Santa knew he did not need to be told this. He remembered the hurt look in Norman eyes. Santa, as a person who was so very interested in making people happy, never wanted to cause the hurt he had caused Norman today. Even though it seemed to Santa at the moment, that Norman was piddling away his time teaching reindeer how to fly and then fixing up a sleigh that Santa would rarely use. Santa knew no matter what the case, it was not ever worth making anyone feel that bad again.

FLYING REINDEER

There was a sense of relief through the North Pole the next day. Everybody had heard that Santa had apologized to Norman and that they had had a big dinner together in Santa's house. The merry hum throughout the workshops was back to normal. The supply issues had been resolved. The elves seemed to be working in harmony, producing toys a little faster than normal. Once again it looked like everything was going to be on schedule for Christmas Eve. When Norman came into the large workshop several days later, to run an errand for Freddy, many elves waved to him and welcomed him in a very cheerful manner. Santa saw this from his workbench and felt relieved.

Norman was back to his normal schedule, giving him plenty of time to work with the animals. He had spent a couple days experimenting with the reindeer. He hitched them to the sleigh in the back room. They understood what he was trying to do. He slid open the large back door. The recent snows of December had left a couple inches of snow on the ground. There was a pathway through the trees where Norman could test the reindeer and sleigh without anybody noticing. Norman had experimented with the reindeer pulling the sleigh. With Prancer as the lead reindeer, it worked fairly well. The first few runs went very smoothly. The next run, Norman placed a few extra feed bags in the sleigh to resemble the weight of Santa himself. After that he added a few more bags of feed to account for the weight of the toys, a full sack of toys to be exact. There did not seem to be any strain for the reindeer.

This morning was the big test. He was going to see if he could get the sleigh to fly along with the reindeer. The message was conveyed from Norman to the reindeer with whatever method of communication they had. The reindeer understood the mission. As they pulled out of the stone barn, the sleigh slid easily as its runners hit the soft snow. The reindeer could sense an energy this morning. The temperature was cold but the sun was bright. The evergreen trees had a white covering of snow. Norman was ready to go. He snapped the reins lightly as Prancer looked back at him from the front of the eight reindeer. The reindeer started trotting across the snow between the trees. As they picked up speed, Prancer rose into the air followed by the rest of the reindeer. The front end of the sleigh lifted off the ground and into the air, bounced one time on the ground and then lifted completely. Soon, Norman was directing the reindeer well above the treetops. He was exhilarated. He had spent the morning applying magic to the sleigh in whatever manner elves apply their magic. He was very pleased with his accomplishments. After a few minutes, he indicated for Prancer to set the sleigh down in an open field a few miles away from the North Pole. Anticipating there would be many places where Santa could not get a running start, Norman wanted to see whether they could get the team of reindeer and the sleigh flying immediately from a standing start. He conveyed this message to the reindeer and this time, with a snap of the reins, the reindeer and the sleigh rose up instantly and then started moving forward into the air.

"Yippeeeee!" Norman yelled, knowing there wasn't anybody around to hear him. The sleigh, with its team of reindeer and its little driver, swooped around and above the treetops for a good length of time before returning to the stable barn. Once there, he unhitched this team of reindeer and gave an extra pile of feed to each of them. He made sure to tell them how much they were loved and what a great job they had done.

NORMAN SAVES CHRISTMAS

For the next few days, Norman attempted to tell Santa what he had put together for him. But unfortunately, because Christmas Eve was very close, everybody was running around in a frenzy. The elves were finishing up the last of the toys. Hector was checking the toys against the list and the many letters that had come in. Santa's magic sack had been filled. It was approaching dusk on Christmas Eve. Norman still had not had the opportunity to show Santa the sleigh and the reindeer. From what it looked like, there was not going to be time. Some of the elves had cleaned out the big wagon. The lanterns and the straps of bells had been placed on the sides of the wagon's seat.

The wagon was being driven toward the front steps where the crowds of elves were congregating. They were waiting to see Santa off on another Christmas Eve expedition. Norman was standing in the crowd waiting to see Santa off like the other elves. He could see Santa showing off another new outfit just inside the front door. Pots of hot chocolate were brought out to the porch, ready to be loaded onto the wagon. The commotion and excitement was growing throughout the crowd of elves. That was when disaster hit. As the team of horses pulled the wagon to the front steps, all of a sudden there was a loud cracking noise. Both of the back wooden spoke wheels broke in two or three places. The big wagon had been used to haul large logs back to the workshop area. Those logs had been cut up to make lumber for some new houses as well as wood pieces for toys. Unfortunately, with the new frenzy of activity from the additional letters, all efforts had been put into making toys. The maintenance of the heavily worked wagon had been put by the wayside.

As both back wheels broke at the same time, the back end of the wagon sank very close to the ground. Everybody looked at the wagon in horror. Santa came rushing out onto the porch. His heart sank as he saw the condition of the back wheels. He knew they could be repaired, but it would take many hours. The crowd fell silent. The elves looked at each other trying to decide what to do. Bobbitt inspected the wheels. He looked up at Santa from behind the wagon and said, "These wheels are finished. We have spare wheels to replace them but we are looking at two or three hours of work."

THE LESSON OF THE NORTH POLE

Why is the North Pole such a happy place? There is a very important message that can be learned from the history of the North Pole. While Santa is sleeping after his long trek on Christmas Eve, the elves have already begun to work on toys for the next year. Hammers are tapping, saws are sawing, paintbrushes are brushing paint, but behind the constant clatter of toy-making, there is the sound of happy elves. Santa's workshop has the underlying musical background noise of humming and singing by the elves.

Why are the elves always so happy? Because just like Santa, they have felt great joy in making toys that are going to make children happy around the world. It has been shown many times that kindness and giving to others is much more rewarding then receiving. This has been taught by many important men and women throughout the world's history. Santa Claus experienced great joy when he discovered how happy his toys made others feel. Mrs. Claus did not eat all the candy she made. Her joy came from knowing that others enjoyed her candy.

Santa thought it was important, every year, to have a list of children that were naughty or nice. Being nice was very important to him. He knew that being nice to other people provided great happiness. You probably know people who are very nice. They like to do things for others without expecting to be paid or gaining recognition. They keep the spirit of Christmas with them the whole year. Everyone has the opportunity to make life better for the people around them, whether it is their parents, their brothers and sisters, their teachers, neighbors or their friends. Giving comes in different forms, such as mentoring, donating time, as well as possessions.

From the very first Christmas, Santa delivered toys to families and children he knew would enjoy their new presents. He did not do it for money. He did not do it for fame. He did it because he discovered the great happiness he experienced by bringing smiles and laughter to others. Isn't this the way everybody should lead their lives?

Isn't it exciting to wake up on Christmas morning to find presents underneath the tree?

Wouldn't it be nice if everyone could experience the excitement of opening presents on Christmas morning. Unfortunately, there are many children in the world who do not have presents to open. This is an opportunity for everybody to be one of Santa's helpers. Wouldn't you feel happy if you made Christmas a happy time for a less fortunate family or child?

As we all get older, it can be clearly seen that there is great excitement and joy for those people who like to give presents to others without expecting to receive presents in return. The Christmas season brings out a spirit in everyone. Family and friends travel far and wide to be together during the holidays. Being together is what makes the holidays so festive. The crackling fire in the fireplace, the lit candles on the mantle, and the sounds of Christmas music throughout the house provides the atmosphere everyone looks forward to each year, knowing they will be together with the ones they love, whether in person or through memories. Make your own memories pleasant by trying a little giving.

These joyous occasions were started by Santa's spirit of giving. That festive spirit remains year-round at the North Pole. As soon as Santa returns with his empty sleigh on Christmas night, the elves get ready to start making toys for the next year. If Santa and his elves are happy throughout the year, think how happy you would be by giving and helping others all year long!